BETWEEN DANCERS

Inside, Doug shook hands with my parents. Then they all glanced toward me in the doorway. Doug lifted his hand in a stiff unsmiling salute and disappeared into the entrance hall. Should I go after him? What was the use?

I returned to the patio and listened for the roar of Doug's car or, perhaps, for the sound of his horn that long ago used to toot twice in farewell. But the disco was too loud. What a terrible night! First, no apprenticeship. Now, no Doug.

Well, I would show him. I would dance with every man here. But on my way back to the party, I tripped on my long green skirt, stumbled on the steps, and would have fallen except for someone who had caught me around the waist. It was Armando.

Other Avon Flare Books by
Karen Strickler Dean

MAGGIE ADAMS' DANCER
MARIANA

Between Dances
Maggie Adams'
Eighteenth Summer

Karen Strickler Dean

AN AVON  FLARE BOOK

BETWEEN DANCES: MAGGIE ADAMS' EIGHTEENTH
SUMMER is an original publication of Avon Books. This work
has never before appeared in book form.

AVON BOOKS
A division of
The Hearst Corporation
1790 Broadway
New York, New York 10019

Library of Congress Cataloging in Publication Data

Dean, Karen Strickler.
  Between dances.

  (An Avon/Flare book)
  Summary: Maggie Adams is torn between her career as
a ballet dancer and her pending marriage.
  [1. Ballet dancing—Fiction] 2. Marriage—Fiction]
I. Title
PZ7.D3443Be   [Fic]   81-22784
ISBN 0-380-79285-0   AACR2

First Flare Printing, May, 1982

FLARE BOOKS TRADEMARK REG. U. S. PAT. OFF. AND IN
OTHER COUNTRIES, MARCA REGISTRADA, HECHO EN U.S.A.

Printed in the U.S.A.

WFH   10   9   8   7   6

For Nathan

Chapter One

To the sweet sounds of Chopin, I eased my knees into a *demi-plié* and began what would be my very last ballet class as a student if I got an apprenticeship in the company. If. If. If. The little word nagged inside my head. I brushed wisps of my red hair back from my forehead.

"You're frowning, Maggie," whispered Lupe beside me at the *barre*. "Is your ankle bothering you?"

She pointed to the elastic bandage and Saran Wrap around my left ankle.

"That's only a precaution. My left foot's weaker, is the one I hurt before. It just feels overworked. No, what's bothering me is my conference after class. They have to give me an apprenticeship, Lupe! Today's my birthday. Dear God, I'm eighteen, the age dancers usually turn professional, if they're ever going to!"

"Old lady Maggie!" said Paul, who also worked next to me, he on one side, Lupe on the other. "Of course, you'll get an apprenticeship. You were top student in our graduating class even before your beautiful *Nocturne* last night. And, hey, happy birthday!"

"Thanks, Paul. Incidentally, congratulations on your apprenticeship. And Lupe's sure to get one. But the way Randall hates me, I'm keeping my fingers crossed."

"*Ojalá*, we all get apprenticeships!" Lupe said.

The fringes of her dark lashes fluttered against her

high Indian cheekbones. She pressed her hand between her small breasts where, under the blue leotard, I knew her St. Christopher medal dangled.

"'And don't worry about Randall, *cariña*. He's only one of four who'll decide."

As if Lupe had conjured him up, Larry Randall, the assistant director of the City Ballet Company, materialized in the doorway. He leaned on his gold-knobbed stick and surveyed us. His gaze finally stopped on me. He seemed to analyze each movement, each muscle, each position of my head, arms, shoulders, torso, legs, feet. Even my fingers.

When the exercise ended, our teacher, Eleanora Martina, glanced up from the canvas chair where she usually sat to teach. Three years ago tendonitis in both knees forced her to retire. Looking at Randall now, she smoothed down her black chiffon skirt. Her gentle voice sounded cold.

"Pray, come in, Mr. Randall."

"Why, thank you, dear, but I can see beautifully from here. And don't let me interrupt your class. I simply wish to check one last time before we give out the remaining apprenticeships tonight."

The remaining apprenticeships! I shivered. I pushed at my hair and crossed my fingers. Dear God, let me do everything perfectly tonight!

Randall soon moved with that loose-hipped walk of his to the front of the room. There, with his back to the mirrors, he assumed the third ballet position, making it look arrogant because of the haughty tilt of his handsome profile and the lift of his shapely blond head.

"By the way, Madame, do your students always take class shrouded in leg warmers and draped with sweaters? Kindly remove them, ladies and gentlemen, so that I may appreciate the lines of your bodies, which, after all, are the instruments of your art."

Stripping off my sweater and woolen leg warmers, I hung them over the *barre*. But Randall wasn't satisfied.

"And, you with the red hair, take off all that Saran Wrap and bandaging. It's totally useless and makes a thick bulge where your ankle should be slim."

Biting my lips to try to control my temper, I did as he asked.

"You see, Lupe! He hates me far too much to give me an apprenticeship. And it was he who refused to partner me in our little regional company's *Nutcracker Ballet*. Not the other way around!"

"Maggie, honey, that was four whole years ago!"

"Yes. But something else happened last Christmas. I really got mad when he was three hours late starting rehearsal. So I walked out."

"My word," Randall said. "Do you allow all this whispering, Madame? You would think this was an adolescent hangout, not a ballet class."

Martina shot him a cold look and began calling out steps for the next exercise. Fortunately, my body was moving easily, as effortlessly tonight as during last night's graduation performance. I got through all the *barre* work beautifully and also the center floor *adagios*.

When Martina switched from *adagios* to *pirouettes*, however, I crossed my fingers because sometimes I teeter on the endings. But not tonight. Securely balanced, I finished each *pirouette*, whether triple or quadruple, in perfect position, in precise tempo.

She went on to a combination of quick little beats and tricky jumps that required all my concentration. Forgetting Randall, I watched and counted while Martina pantomimed the steps.

"Think you have it, Maggie, Lupe? Good. Then please demonstrate for the others."

"But, Madame," I began, hanging back.

Lupe excelled at these steps, while I, being taller and slimmer, was better at variations which displayed my line. The *arabesques* and *développés* in last night's *Nocturne*, for instance. Randall was sure to compare us.

"No buts, Maggie," Madame said.

Lupe and I took the starting position and, when the music began, we both sprang into the first *entrechat-six*. Reflected beside me in the mirror, she flew, hovered like a hummingbird, but I looked almost as nimble. I fluttered my pointed feet, leaped, glided, soared. Suddenly, I felt myself lifted by the exhilaration, the same joy of dancing that long ago—when I was a student down the Peninsula at McMichael's Ballet School—I named my summer wind.

After Lupe and I finished the entire variation, Randall merely raised an eyebrow, but the students in the class applauded.

Then it was their turn. Lupe and I retired to the *barre* at the back of the room to rest and to watch. She glanced sideways at me from the tilted corners of her brown eyes. She laid a hand on my arm.

"I saw Randall looking at you, *cariña*. He couldn't help but be impressed. You're good at everything—lyrical combinations, and, now, he'll know you're an allegro dancer, too."

"Hey, you're right, Lupe," said Paul, whose group had not yet been called up to dance the combination.

"Thanks. I hope so."

Then, seeing Randall look our way, I stopped whispering and watched the other students.

In the first group, directly in front of Randall, danced

Kathy, the first friend I made after entering this school three years ago. To perform the variation, she needed to cross the spot where he stood. But he wouldn't move. So Kathy had to weave now to his right, then to his left. Her usually clean technique faltered in the *brisés* and she finally fell apart, jerking this way and that, like a poorly manipulated puppet.

When the next group moved forward, Kathy limped to a *barre* clear across on the opposite side of the room from us. There she pressed her face into her towel, and, I'm sure, began to cry. Her pale hair slid in damp wisps down from the tight topknot at the crown of her head. Poor Kathy!

All the other students managed Martina's *allegro* combination fairly well. Even Paul. His inflexible feet, when required to beat, tended to flap like a pelican's wings rather than whir like a hummingbird's. He got through the variation, however, by changing the *entrechats* to simple *royales* and by not beating the *brisés*.

After a few more combinations, which, thank heavens, Randall watched without comment, Martina called for *grands battements* from second position, signaling the end of class. But while the old pianist's veined and yellowed hands searched for the music, Randall rapped his cane on the floor.

"One minute. One minute. Excuse me, Madame. But, of course, your students are accustomed to your combinations. In the company, however—should any of them be fortunate enough to be accepted someday—they will have to work with other teachers, other choreographers. I don't mean to take over your class, dear, but please allow me to give your students a variation very different from yours."

Oh, no! But Martina bowed and stepped back. She had to let him take over her exhausted class.

"Pray, be my guest!"

He returned her bow and then the show-off circled with pointed toes and a flourish of hands as if he were performing Cavalier, the role in *Nutcracker* he had refused to dance with me four years ago.

"As some of you are painfully aware, ladies and gentlemen, I demand absolute precision. When I say fifth position, I mean precisely fifth, not some aberration halfway between third and fourth. And when I say *effacée*, I mean precisely *effacée*. This is what I want now. *Effacée*."

His nasal voice rattled off a list of steps while he pranced through them, pounding the tempo with his stick. My stomach tightened, but while Randall shouted instructions to the pianist, my mind reviewed the steps and my hands pantomimed them.

"All right, ladies and gentlemen. I want three lines. In front, Lupe. Then over here, Paul. Next to Seth. Yes, Paul, don't be so shy. Pull up that fine long body of yours and stand with pride. Use Seth as your model. Yes, of course, I want you in the front row. But, for heaven's sake, don't clench your fists. There's no need to be so nervous. You and Seth are apprentices now. Then the young lady with the red hair. Didn't you use to wear braces on your teeth, dear? What's your name? Oh, yes, Maggie Adams. Right here, Maggie Adams."

So he did remember me, the fourteen-year-old kid with a mouthful of braces! But I couldn't think about that now. I had to keep reviewing his steps. For I knew that Randall wouldn't repeat them. The egotist prided himself on showing a combination only once.

After Martina's lovely floating variations, his was a military drill. But it was simple. Thank heavens, it was simple when we were all so tired. You only had to dance with precision. Which I did.

12

Feet wedged into an exact fifth, body faced exactly *effacée*, I shot into Randall's combination. To the beat of his stick, *sissone, sissone*, across the floor, *pas de bourrée, brisé, brisé, assemblé*. Now the other side, but pressing the floor before soaring into the second *brisé*, I felt a slight pull. Dear God! My Achilles tendon. I had to stop. If I went on, I might really hurt it, rupture it even. He should never have made me remove the Saran Wrap.

Grasping my left ankle, I limped out of the other students' path. Oh, but what about the apprenticeship now?

Randall's cane hit the floor. The music ceased.

"Why did you stop, Maggie Adams? On stage, dancers never stop. Never. Even if they're seriously injured, even if they fracture something, they keep dancing. But you, sweet Jesus, you stopped cold, limped away. Like this, like a lizard dragging its tail."

Exaggerating my limp, he lurched forward on one foot, trailing the other behind.

"Terrible! All right. We'll do it again. Everybody. Including Maggie Adams. Especially Maggie Adams."

"No. I can't. I'm afraid I might rupture the tendon."

"Nonsense. Take your place at once!"

"No, Mr. Randall."

He glared at me, spun on his heel, and forced the rest of the class, including Kathy, to repeat his hideous variation. When he ended, he shrugged dramatically.

"Well, ladies and gentlemen, what can I say? And then you wonder why we give so few apprenticeships!"

Moving toward the door, he whirled suddenly and, using his stick like a foil, poked it toward Lupe.

"You, girl, follow me downstairs for your conference."

Lupe's eyes widened.

"Yes, you. Now. *Muy pronto*, as you say in Mexican."

After he left, Lupe turned to Martina.

"*Por dios!* Right now? Can't I change first?"

"No, go on, Lupe. And don't worry. I'll be right down."

Lupe looked over to where I stood at the *barre*, keeping my weight off my left foot. I tried to smile. I waved my crossed fingers at her.

"You'll get one, Lupe!"

"Oh, you too, *cariña*."

She picked up her ballet bag from among those left near the door and started out, only to be almost run down by Randall who was back again. This time his stick pointed at me.

"And you, Maggie Adams. You're after Lupe. So get yourself downstairs, one way or another."

Chapter Two

After Randall left a second time, Martina came over and with careful fingers, felt along my tendon.

"It seems all right, Maggie. Just a bit strained maybe from too many classes and rehearsals. But at least it got you through the Gala last night. I'll see you downstairs in a few minutes."

My answer was a long sigh.

I leaned against the *barre*, my back to it, my elbows resting on it. So now it was over, ended, the very last ballet class of the season. But would the ending also be a beginning, as the speakers said last week at my high school commencement? That depended on my conference.

I looked around the studio, something I hadn't done all the time we were taking technique exams and rehearsing for our Gala. I saw the fluorescent ceiling tubes reflected in the mirrors. I noticed how wan Martina looked limping out the door. I watched the students, including small ginger-haired Seth and my friends Kathy and Paul, collect from the long *barres* their laundry of sweaters, leg warmers, and old musty towels.

"Hey, Maggie, it's finally over!" Paul said, coming up with Kathy. "How's the ankle?"

"Okay. I just didn't want to take the chance of really hurting it."

"Well, I'll carry you downstairs anyway. Just in case."

15

"Don't be silly. I can manage. But I wish Randall would give me time to get dressed and comb my hair. It's frizzing all over the place."

"Your hair's beautiful. Such a pretty pale shade. Tangerine."

"Tangerine!" Kathy said, lounging against the *barre*, giving a snort of laughter. "Whooee! How poetic! How about her eyes? Let's see: green as hidden mountain pools. Commonly known as fish-pond green."

"Oh, shut up, Kathy!" I said. "We're all tired and worried about the apprenticeships. They just have to give me one!"

"Do they?" she asked sharply. I looked at her. She was an old friend, so why the stinging question? Then I knew.

"You didn't get one, Kathy! Why didn't you tell us? I'm really sorry. You deserve one."

Paul said, "It's awfully unfair."

"You're right, absolutely right," Kathy said.

Her usual blond pertness was gone. Her voice wobbled.

"It's terribly, terribly unfair. I've studied ten years, ten long years, but because the company wants boys, I don't get an apprenticeship."

"Hey, I guess you're blaming me," Paul said.

"No. It's just the whole shitty dance racket. Because of the shortage of male dancers, a boy can start studying really late, say sixteen, seventeen, eighteen, and after two or three years of lessons get an apprenticeship like you did, Paul."

"I don't blame you for feeling cheated," Paul said. "You're a much better dancer than I'll ever be. So is Maggie."

"What'll I do if I don't get one?" I wailed. "Ballet's my whole life!"

Kathy gave another snort which was more like a sob than a laugh.

16

"It's not exactly a hobby with me either! Anyway, I'm splitting, ducking out. Out of everything. Including your birthday party tonight, Maggie. I hope you don't mind. I'm going straight home to bed. Besides, lately, I've been getting the feeling that you two would just as soon not have me tagging along."

I stared after Kathy, who skittered off down the corridor, loose-ankled, feet angled out, her near-white hair clinging like wet straw to her neck and shoulders.

"What's with her?" I asked. "What's she talking about?"

But when I looked at Paul for an explanation, I got the crazy feeling that his blue, clear eyes were filmed over with thin, inner lids like those of my canary at home. The film shut me out, kept me from seeing what he was really thinking.

"What's Kathy talking about, Paul?"

"How should I know?"

"I mean, we're all friends. So why did she rush off like that? I think maybe she likes you, Paul. A lot. But even if she does, why should she be jealous of me?"

"I said I don't know what's bugging Kathy. I really don't. Sometimes, though, Maggie, I sort of wish you'd, well, notice me for myself, not as just a partner, you know."

"But I do notice you, Paul. You're one of my best friends. A brother."

"Hey, I'm not talking about being a brother. I guess I'm not very good at explaining. I mean, I never had much to do with girls at home. My mother always said they just get you into trouble. But I get really mixed up thinking about you, Maggie. And I can't get you out of my mind."

"Paul, we're friends, just friends. So let's drop the sub-

17

ject, okay? Are you still coming to my birthday party to-night?"

"As a matter of fact, Maggie, I can't. I found out that Larry Randall is giving a dinner for all the new apprentices. And, hey, Maggie, please forget what I said. You're right. We're friends, period. And I'm sorry I can't come to your party."

Although I liked Paul, I wasn't sorry he couldn't come because Doug would be there. Actually, he was picking me up here after my conference and driving me home. I hadn't seen much of him since he went away to Berkeley two years ago, but I thought we could get reacquainted easier without Paul along.

Paul also seemed relieved not to be coming. When he handed me my ballet bag, he was his relaxed friendly self again. And his eyes were clear.

"You'd better put on leg warmers, Maggie. And a sweater too. Then I'll carry you downstairs."

"I told you, I'm okay. I can walk."

"No way. Besides, I want to do it."

He picked me up and carried me through the corridor, down the stairs, and into the foyer, where people were letting in cold breaths of San Francisco fog every time they entered or left. We stopped outside the red lacquered door of the school director's office. Against the white-washed wall glistened the leaves of a plastic rubber plant.

"Think you can stand up, Maggie? Try putting your weight on your bad foot. Hey, easy does it!"

"Paul, stop worrying. I'm perfectly all right. Look."

I shifted onto my left foot. I took a practice step, then another.

"Not even a twinge. Believe me, I'm fine. But thanks. How long do you think I'll have to wait for my conference?"

Before he could answer my question, the door opened and out came Lupe. Seeing us, she rushed into our arms.

"I got one, Maggie! Oh, Paul, I got an apprenticeship!"

"Terrific, Lupe," I said.

I was happy for her. But an ugly doubt stung me. If she and Paul received apprenticeships and Kathy didn't, what were my chances?

"Hey, that's great news, Lupe," Paul said. "And you deserve one. So hardworking, so talented. And those jumps of yours and little beats are out of this world."

Like most theatre people, dancers touch each other a lot so we hugged and patted until the door swung open again. Within its frame lounged Larry Randall.

"Well, Maggie Adams, I'm glad to see that you were able to get yourself down here on that injured foot of yours. Now if you can drag yourself away from your friends. Unless, of course, you want your conference staged out here before the entire company, the school, and any parents or strangers who happen to wander out of the San Francisco fog and into our bright and friendly foyer."

I felt like saying, "Oh, shut up, you big windbag," but Paul said, "Better go in."

When I slid past Randall, he drew aside his lean elegant body as if to touch me might give him some terrible disease. He bowed me into the ten-by-twelve white cell that served as the school director's office.

On one wall was thumbtacked last season's publicity poster of Linda Larson, a company soloist, silhouetted against a midnight blue background.

Randall followed me into the office, where he settled onto a high wobbly stool and twined his long legs around each other like thick vines. Behind his desk, Terrence Chagall, director of the school, crossed and recrossed his knees. His long thigh muscles identified him also as a dancer. He cleared his throat.

"Well, Maggie, here we all are, waiting to have a little chat with you. You know everybody, don't you? Robert Morris, our company director."

I nodded to this small neat man with wiry gray hair and electric blue eyes. A former dancer, he sat quietly in a director's chair with one loafered foot hooked across the thigh of his other leg.

"And, of course, you know my wife."

From where she perched on a tall stool, my teacher Martina gave me her beautiful smile, but then her glance went nervously from face to face.

"And Larry Randall, our assistant director."

Randall tilted his movie-star profile and smoothed his yellow hair, which always looked painted on because he used so much hair spray.

"Maggie and I have been acquainted since she wore braces on her teeth. Since she knows everybody here, Terry, let's just explain our new policy and get on with it. I'm giving a dinner party tonight and want to get away early."

"We'll do our best to accommodate you, Larry," Chagall said, but a flush darkened his tanned face to the color of redwood. "However, I'd like to do this my way."

"By all means, Terry. You're headmaster. Fortunately. Because I want nothing to do with ballet schools, this one, or the prestigious one across town. I detest frog-legged baby dancers and giggly adolescent females with budding chests and braces on their teeth."

I bristled, felt my face heat up, jabbed the floor with the *pointe* of my right foot, and wanted to retort: Those females you despise so much, you chauvinist, are the future dancers of this country!

20

I resisted, however, because this conference, after all, could mean the end or the beginning of my ballet career.

"That's why I leave most of the teaching to you, Terry and Elly, and, of course, to Lermontov," Randall went on. "Now and then, though, I do enjoy taking over a boys' class because that's where the challenge really is in this backward country of ours: the need to provide a sufficient number of well-trained male dancers."

"Yes, of course, Larry, but let's get on with this conference, particularly since you're in such a hurry. Maggie, we're very pleased with your progress and think you show extraordinary talent. Your *Nocturne* last night was enchanting. But, because we're trying to strengthen the male contingent of City Ballet Company, we're taking only male apprentices this year with the exception of one girl."

The room grew absolutely silent. I could hear the silence. It hung like the fog that covered the city outside. One girl. And I knew that girl was Lupe, sweet little Lupe, my best friend. But I must be mistaken.

"Are—are you telling me I'm not getting an apprenticeship?"

"I'm afraid so, Maggie."

Dear God, I felt so shaky. My throat clogged up. I must have paled too, because Martina left her stool and pushed it toward me. Her voice echoed from wall to wall, sounded far away.

"Oh, honey, you'll get one next year. Here, sit down."

"No, thank you, Madame, I'll—I'll stand."

I tried to control the wobble in my voice, push back my tears because I refused to cry in front of Randall. Also I refused to accept their decision, his decision.

"Isn't this sex discrimination, Mr. Randall? Because I'm certainly one of the two or three top dancers in the graduating class. My exams show that. Then I was given the *Nocturne* in the Gala, danced it okay, beautifully, everybody says."

"Didn't we say you are very promising?" Randall asked. "As Madame says, you'll probably receive an apprenticeship next year. After all, what's one year? As for discriminating, no. Haven't we chosen one female?"

"A token female!"

"Hardly. Your little Mexican friend, Lupe Herrera, received the one apprenticeship allotted to a female this year. You would have difficulty defending a discrimination charge when our one girl apprentice is a minority female like Lupe."

"I'm not objecting to Lupe getting an apprenticeship. She's very talented, but so am I, not to mention Kathy and lots of others."

"Maggie's right," Martina said. "Or, if this ridiculous, shortsighted policy allows us only one girl, Maggie should be that girl. As I've pointed out till I'm blue in the face, she has the makings of a fine classical dancer. On the other hand, Lupe, despite her quick clean technique, is so tiny that she'll be limited to certain specialty roles. Also I'm afraid she lacks the necessary physical strength and endurance after her illness a few years ago."

"Excuse me, Madame," I said, "but what you say is not true. Lupe's tiny but she projects beautifully. As for not being strong, my father believes that she made a complete recovery from the anorexia nervosa. He was her doctor, you know."

"Ladies! Ladies! This is no time to argue," Randall said. "We chose Lupe Herrera because the company needs her type to fill the vacancy left when Linda Larson took it into her head to go off and get pregnant. And, as far as I know, Lupe has no chronic injury such as a strained Achilles tendon."

"So that's why. My tendon. But it's okay. Just a little tired from all the exams and rehearsals. All it needs is rest."

I brushed a lock of hair off my forehead. Why hadn't I kept on dancing after I felt the twinge in class tonight? But the apprenticeships must have been decided on weeks ago. Now Randall slid off his stool.

"Really, Elly, Terry, everybody. Our decision has been made, according to our new company policy. I'm sorry Maggie is disappointed, but she's not the first to be, or the last. Now I really must run."

He strode out. Robert Morris followed, but paused briefly in the doorway. "Next year, Maggie," he said.

Chapter Three

I stared at the red lacquered door which Randall and Morris had closed behind them. My throat ached.

"Oh, damn that Randall!"

"Randall's a bastard, all right," Martina said, putting her arms around me.

"All the same, hang in there, Maggie," Chagall said. He patted me on the back.

"Oh, hang in there yourself!" Martina cried. "Why did you knuckle under to them? Couldn't you stand up to that pair for once?"

Shoving his hands into the pockets of his slacks, Chagall shrugged and turned away.

"I only work here."

Martina gave me her handkerchief and led me to the door.

"It's a rotten shame, Maggie. But try to have a good holiday anyway."

At the door she handed me over to Lupe and Paul, who apparently read the bad news on my face.

"Oh, *por dios! Por dios!* I feel so guilty. How come I got an apprenticeship and you didn't, *cariña*, when you're a much better dancer?"

"I don't want to talk about it, Lupe. If I do, I'll cry. And I don't want Doug to see me all red-eyed. And, oh, my party! I almost forgot about that. I sure don't feel like a party tonight!"

"Neither do I," Paul said. "Especially not Randall's. The way he sort of pranced out of Chagall's office just now, waved at me, called in that high, affected voice I really hate, 'See you in an hour at my place, Paul. Don't forget now!' Lord! Hey, Maggie, I won't go! I'll come down to your party instead, if that's all right. How about you, Lupe? Are you going to Randall's party for the new apprentices?"

"Not me. I wasn't even invited. Anyway, me and Eddy, we're going to a sort of party down in San Jose. But maybe we could stop by to say 'Happy birthday' on our way, Maggie. If that's okay?"

"Fine."

I looked at them, my two best friends. What was wrong with me not to care whether Lupe and her Eddy stopped by? Not to want Paul driving down with Doug and me?

"Sure, Lupe, please come. I want to meet this Eddy you're always talking about."

She blushed, ducked her head, giggled. Her eyelashes fluttered above the long bridge of her slightly convex Indian nose.

"He's nice, Maggie. He's a friend of my brother. Or used to be."

Her voice suddenly grew husky but quickly returned to normal.

"His name's really Edwardo, but I call him Eddy. You'll really like him."

"I'm sure. And, if he's a friend of your brother, he must be serious about you."

"Well, yes. At least, I hope so."

"But, Paul," I said, turning to him. "You'd better not miss Randall's dinner or he'll have it in for you, just like he does for me."

"I could say I was sick."

26

"He won't believe you."

"Hey, but I am sick—sick of all the personalities and politics around here."

I sighed. I wasn't sick, just tired and discouraged. But, at least, I would soon see Doug.

"You have to go, Paul. You can't be like me, battling Randall all the time. Or you'll end up being dismissed after your apprenticeship, never becoming a full-fledged member of the company."

"I guess you're right, Maggie. I'll call you tomorrow then, okay? Bye, Lupe. And, hey, have a great time with Eddy."

After he left, Lupe and I went to the women's dressing room, where the air hung dense with the odors of baby powder and sweat. Only a few dancers remained sitting along the wooden benches. Some were dressing. Others rested, thin and naked, against the cold plaster walls.

But Lupe hurried, sponged her small brown body, hooked on a black lace bra, buckled up her three-inch heeled sandals, slid into a flame-red nylon dress. For she had things to celebrate: both a sweetheart and an apprenticeship.

I tried to close my mind to everything except Doug. I wondered how he looked, if he would kiss me hello, what would happen between us now that he had this summer job in Silicon Valley, close to where I lived.

I changed quickly into my jeans and pullover and was putting on high-heeled sandals when Kathy leaned in at the door.

"A couple of men are out in the foyer looking for you, Maggie and Lupe."

Lupe jumped up. Her eyes shone. She pulled a comb through her long thick hair, then leaned down to hug me where I sat fastening my sandals.

"See you later. And, *cariña*, I'm really sorry about the apprenticeship! You really should have mine."

She was out the door before I could answer. But looking after her, I met Kathy's white-lashed, pink-bordered eyes.

"I thought you went home to bed, Kathy."

"Well, no. I haven't had the energy to get going yet. And, Maggie, honestly, you should have had an apprenticeship. Paul just told me the bad news."

Then a quick smile brought back some of her scrubbed blond prettiness. "You do have one consolation: he's really something, that man waiting for you out in the foyer."

Suddenly nervous, wondering if seeing Doug would be as exciting as I expected, I went to the dressing room door. Looking out, I saw Lupe smiling up at a short well-built man. His muscles stretched out the shoulders of his dark jacket. His hair met at the back in a pair of shiny blackbird wings. His face was brown and hawk-nosed. I heard Lupe's hesitant little voice.

"Hi, Eddy. Like my new dress?"

"I guess so, honey, but it's a bit too bright. Anyway, let's get out of here."

Smiling, he clamped an arm around her narrow shoulders and propelled her out the door. What a heel to say that about the dress she was so proud of! But then I saw Doug. And the old excitement did jolt me as much as ever.

Doug stood near the door through which Lupe and Eddy had disappeared. His curly blond head reached nearly to the acoustical tiles and fluorescent tubes on the ceiling. Among the small dancers, he looked as if he belonged to another species, another planet.

Something was different about him. A beard. Good

heavens, a neatly trimmed beard and mustache screened his upper lip and chin. Then I started to giggle. I couldn't help it because his beard wasn't dark blond like his own curling hair. It was red, pale red like my hair.

Laughing, shaking my tangled mass of hair free of bobby pins, combs, nets, rubber bands, I rushed out to him. It was like seeing him that very first time when I was a mere high school freshman and he a lofty junior showing our group around the school. To me, he resembled a Greek god, then and now.

"Doug! Hello! I don't believe it. Your beard. Your red beard!"

In the midst of it, his full tender mouth opened in a laugh showing those beautiful teeth I used to admire so much, particularly when mine were still behind braces.

Now he lifted me up by the elbows, swung me around, but he didn't kiss me before he set me down. Maybe because the foyer was so public.

"Right, Mag! Isn't it amazing? What a surprise! Out it grew—red! Reminding me of you. So now we're practically twins. Gosh, it's good to see you. And happy birthday! You're looking great. Somehow taller though. More graceful. More grown-up, I guess. Your head comes almost to my chin now."

"It's the high heels. I'm still only five-feet-five, but for a dancer that's plenty tall enough."

Doug continued to smile down at me, apparently as glad to see me as I was to see him.

"How are you anyway, Mag?"

"Fine!"

Which, at the moment, I was. Seeing him standing there—tall, blond, athletic—made me forget my problems and remember our times together. Especially the picnic by the lake where he kissed me for the first time.

And now he had a red beard! Laughing, I touched it, soft, curly, tickling my hand.

Then—while I was being so silly, so stupid about the beard, about Doug, from behind the plastic rubber plant or from among the people crowding the foyer; or maybe just from beside him and I had been too dazzled to notice anyone but Doug; anyway, from somewhere—this girl appeared. Doug introduced her finally, one of those long-haunched, big-boobed, statuesque, plastic-type dollies he used to date in high school when ballet didn't spare me enough time for him.

"Mag, this is Charmaine. Charmaine, Maggie Adams."

"Hi."

"Hello."

I could swear she inched her cashmere-sweatered shoulders forward above her ballooning breasts in a bored, frozen shrug. And wouldn't you know her name would be Charmaine! Her glassy, gold-flecked, vacant eyes regarded me from beneath shiny blue lids and lashes dragging with mascara. I stared back, feeling my face grow hot while Doug explained why he had brought another girl along on what I considered a date. Though, of course, it was only after my mother invited him to my birthday party that he called up and offered me a ride.

"Charmaine lives in my dorm, Mag, and she needed a ride down to Foster City tonight. So, of course, I said I'd drop her off."

"Of course."

"You see, Charmaine, I told you Maggie wouldn't mind."

Doug wrapped a friendly arm around my shoulders, hugging me as if he were rewarding the birthday girl for sharing her favorite toy with the company. Of course, he was free to date whom he pleased. We certainly had exchanged no promises; hardly ever saw each other anymore. But Charmaine!

Slipping out of his grasp, I made for the front door in my high-heeled sandals and rolled-up jeans, trying to forget the elegant drape of her cashmere skirt and the softness of her high leather boots. Why hadn't I brought along the green silk dress I planned to wear to my party?

"We might as well get started," I called back to Doug. "I'm really exhausted from class and everything."

I pushed through one of the heavy glass doors, letting the fog cool my face and body. Not only had I lost an apprenticeship, but Doug. I had lost Doug.

I angled ahead of them toward the corner where the traffic lights glowed, turned the icy fog into different flavored sherbets: now lime, then orange, then raspberry.

"Wait, Mag! Not that way!" Doug called. "I'm parked in the lot across the street."

I returned to where Doug waited for me on the curb beside Charmaine; then went ahead of them between the parked cars. I heard someone call me. Not Doug this time. No—from the door of the ballet school came Paul's voice with a strange shake in it.

"Maggie. Hey, Maggie!"

I stopped in the middle of the street and waited near Doug and his Charmaine.

"Who is it?" Doug asked.

"A friend of mine from the ballet school."

Then Paul rushed up, panting, his face long and pale, a lock of light brown hair concealing his eyes.

"Paul, is something wrong?"

"No. Not really. But for a minute I was afraid you had already gone, Maggie. I wonder, I mean, is it all right if I take you up on your offer of a ride down to your party?

31

The dinner didn't work out after all. Excuse me," he added to Doug, "do you mind if I come along? Do you have room?"

I introduced everybody, and standing in the middle of the street, Paul and Doug shook hands.

Earlier I had not wanted Paul along, but now with Charmaine here, I welcomed him. I took one of his arms.

"Of course, please do come, Paul. It's all right, isn't it, Doug? I mean, the more, the merrier!"

Chapter Four

Doug's car turned out to be some sort of little foreign model, bright orange, with two bucket seats in front, separated by the gear shift. The back seat, reached by folding down a front seat, consisted of a shelf and a narrow trough. The designers had not thought to provide enough space for legs, particularly not for the legs of dancers, which really must be stretched out after ballet class to avoid aches and cramps.

"What happened to your big car, Doug?"

"Same old Mag. You never did notice cars, did you? This was my graduation present. Don't you remember going to the park and to Santa Cruz in it the summer after I graduated from high school? When ballet didn't interfere, that is."

He was laughing, teasing me, but at least he remembered. Maybe we would still be going together if he hadn't spent last summer away in Montana working on oil rigs. But now I wondered how we would all position ourselves in his little car.

As Doug's date, if I was Doug's date, I should, of course, sit up front with him and let Paul and long-haunched Charmaine cram themselves into the back. But as I hesitated, Charmaine slid onto the passenger's front bucket seat.

"Oops," she said to Doug with a throaty laugh, "I

guess I should have let them get in back first, shouldn't I? But I'll just scrunch forward so they can crowd past."

I sure wanted to scrunch Charmaine, but while Doug put my ballet bag into the trunk, I followed Paul onto the hard shelf and doubled my legs sideways into the trough.

"Sorry you're so crowded back there," Doug said, climbing into the driver's side. "But it won't be for long. You know how I drive, Mag, with split-second precision!"

Spinning the car out of the parking lot, he twisted through a maze of one-way streets bordered by Victorian row houses. Soon he found a ramp and swooped up onto the Skyway, an elevated freeway.

From there, if you were in the mood to appreciate beauty, the whole lighted city burst forth. Its sleek buildings leaned against a green-black sky. Tonight fog strung out in long boas around the shoulders of the skyscrapers. But I could think only of where I should be sitting right now—up front with Doug.

"How did your finals go, Doug?" I asked, resting my chin on the back of his seat.

"Okay, I guess, Mag. I don't really know yet, but I think I did all right."

"I'm sure you did beautifully," Charmaine cooed—possessively, I thought. "Engineering exams are no picnic, but I think studying together all those nights really helped, don't you, Dougy?"

"How nice that you two have something in common," I said.

Nice? Well, hardly. And she certainly wasn't. Her words were barbs and meant for me. But "Dougy"? Yuck! I felt like throwing up.

"So you're into engineering too, Charmaine?"

"Oh, yes, but only four classes. I started in with five, but had to drop one. Engineering courses are tough, you know."

"I guess I didn't tell you, Mag. Charmaine's an electrical engineering major, too. I'm only finishing my sophomore year, but she's a junior. And made Phi Beta Kappa in her junior year. Which is really something!"

"Oh."

I mean, what could I say? And Paul was no help at all. He sagged beside me, staring out the window, apparently wrapped up in troubles of his own. I tried to stretch my cramped and aching legs but there wasn't room.

Switching on his tape deck, Doug wove south through the evening traffic on the Bayshore Freeway. His little car devoured the highway, practically flew over it, and I was glad. The faster we went, the sooner I would be rid of Charmaine. And Doug? Yes, because I was afraid he planned to drop off Paul and me at my party and then go somewhere else with Charmaine.

But his plans must be for later. At the Foster City turnoff, he left the Bayshore, swung past a sprawl of shopping centers and into a puzzle of lanes. Which he apparently knew as well or better than he knew the streets in my own neighborhood. He had to ask no directions of Charmaine.

Wood and stucco houses spread across shallow lots along the circling roads and waterways. And all this used to be part of the bay. Now nothing remained of all that lovely water except a system of canals dredged out of the blue sludge in order to provide backyard docks for boating enthusiasts.

Doug stopped in front of a house shingled with redwood. Hooded lamps spotlighted its landscaping of giant ferns and flowering shrubs.

Doug got out, collected Charmaine's luggage from the trunk, and arrived at the passenger's side in time to help her unfold and land her stately legs and torso. Then, of course, he had to carry her suitcases and boxes to her front door, where in the shadows their heads came together.

She must have kissed him, briefly, but right on the mouth, I was sure. Or maybe he kissed her. I couldn't really see. I slid down beside Paul, who put an arm along the back of the seat behind me. Well, about time he was coming to life!

"Hey, how are you doing, Maggie?"

"I don't know, Paul. My legs ache. How about yours?"

I leaned against him just as Doug got back into the car and turned to ask, "Anyone want to come up front?"

"No, thanks. Paul and I are doing just fine back here."

"Oh, go on up there, Maggie, if you want."

"No, That's all right, Paul. The headlights hurt my eyes."

What happened next finally convinced me of Doug's total indifference. If he had muttered something short and sarcastic, slammed the car door, burned rubber when he started away from the curb, I could have believed that he was jealous, that something still existed between us, and not between him and Charmaine. But *no*.

"Well, suit yourselves."

Fifteen minutes later he stopped in front of my house.

Every window and all our outdoor lamps blazed, back-lighting the oak tree, whose branches spread across the front of the house and over our long sloping lawn. Mama had fastened various colored shades on the small wrought-iron lamps that lined the curving driveway. In the darkness they bloomed like flowers.

"Wow, looks like somebody's having a party!" Doug said, opening the door for Paul and me and waiting while we crawled out.

"Well, thanks for the ride, Doug," I said, resigned, expecting him to leave immediately for Foster City and

Charmaine. To my surprise, after getting my bag out of his trunk, he joined Paul and me in climbing the curve of lawn.

Out the open front door spilled yellow light and loud disco music, which was a great concession from my parents. My father liked the syrupy stuff, neither classical nor popular, aired over Radio KABL, and Mama doted on Chopin and Schumann.

In the entry hall she rustled toward us in a long white dress that gleamed with cleverly interwoven silver threads. Her copper-colored hair bounced and curled about her shoulders in a young style she had adopted when she started to college a few years ago. She hugged me.

"Happy birthday, Maggie! Oh, happy birthday, baby!"

"Thanks, Mama. Mama, this is Paul. I've told you about him. And you remember Doug."

"How nice to meet you, Paul. And to see you again, Doug. Though I didn't recognize you with that lovely red beard. I hear you're still at Berkeley."

"Yes, but I've applied to MIT."

"Terrific. I hope you're accepted."

MIT, I thought. Massachusetts Institute of Technology. Wasn't that way back east near Boston? But worry turned to surprise when I saw my mother, not shaking hands with Doug as she had with Paul, but actually kissing him, only on the cheek, of course. And he didn't seem to mind. I wished I had dared. But then, Doug and Mama always got along. It was my father who used to bark at Doug if he and I got home after my twelve o'clock pumpkin hour.

But now when my father came into the hall, he shook hands as heartily with Doug as with Paul.

"Glad you both could come."

Then he seized me in a great bear hug.

"Here you are, home at last! Happy birthday, Mags!"

When he released me, he held me at arm's length.

"And you used to be such a scrawny, ugly little red-headed kid! Just like me in my baby pictures!"

"She never was ugly or scrawny!" Mama cried, her eyes trying to signal me. And I knew what she wanted to ask: Did you get an apprenticeship, baby? But I wouldn't talk about it now, not in front of my father, not until I calmed down and could handle his probing questions. And not with Doug and Paul here. Already they were looking uncomfortable, their glances skirting the room, their feet shifting.

"Mama, would you show Doug and Paul where they can find something to eat? I have to go change my clothes."

In my room I put on the green silk dress that I had worn to my high school graduation a week ago. I hoped Doug would like it. I tied back my hair with a narrow matching scarf, and strapped on new high-heeled pumps. Ankle-breakers, my father called them. Fortunately, my ankle seemed fine again.

Then before I joined the party out on the patio, I looked through the glass wall of the living room and saw friends, mostly from my old ballet school, standing, talking, eating, and dancing on the waxed flagstones under a chain of bright paper lanterns.

Doug and Paul stood near the buffet table eating cold cuts and cheese from paper plates. Their eyes moved over the dancing couples and talking groups. Apparently, they had little to say to each other. I hurried out.

"Well, here I am. Do you like my new dress?"

I whirled so that my long skirt spun out into a full green circle.

"Hey, you look beautiful, Maggie," Paul said. "I like the color. Matches your eyes."

Watching me, Doug only smiled. What was he thinking? I held out my arms.

38

"Who wants to dance?"

"I do," Paul said, "if you're sure your ankle's really okay."

"It feels great."

"All right, then." He put an arm around me and turned courteously to Doug. "If you don't mind?"

"You're the dancer," Doug said, extending one palm in a gesture of giving. Oh, why didn't he object!

Holding me firmly, Paul spun me in a waltz, completely disregarding the disco tune pounding from the stereo. Above us, a faint breeze stirred the colored lanterns and dropped a few oak leaves onto the flagstones. I waved or shouted "Hi" to old friends we passed.

"I can't tell you how really glad I am to be here," Paul said, tightening his hold around my waist. He didn't look at me, stared over my head.

"What happened? Why did you decide to come at the last minute, Paul?"

"Well, I got to talking with Steve and Jim in the dressing room. They got apprenticeships too, you know, Maggie. And they said, hell no, they weren't going to Randall's dinner. You couldn't drag them. Besides, they had dates with a couple of girls they met in a modern dance class at SF State."

"You could still have gone, Paul. Without Jim and Steve you could have made even more points with the boss."

"Hey, not me, Maggie. Without Jim and Steve, that would leave, besides me, only Seth and Randall. And, I suppose, Morris, who's Randall's roommate. All a bunch of gays."

"For heaven's sake, Paul. So what? Of course, Randall's a creep. But Morris is okay. And Seth is really nice —kind of shy, but fun to talk to, really intelligent. I'm glad you came to my party though."

When the tune ended, Paul guided me back to Doug.

"Here she is. I returned her safe and sound."

I held out my arms to Doug, inviting him to dance but he smiled down at me through the screen of his beard. One hand was occupied with a refilled plate, the other with a mug of beer. He jerked his full hands up and down in mock helplessness.

"Can't, Mag. Look, no hands."

"Well, then, if you'll excuse me, I have other guests to attend to."

Forget him! I flounced over to where I saw Joyce dancing with a dark-haired muscular young man not much taller than she. Joyce used to be one of my best friends at McMichael's ballet school in San Jose before she gave up dancing and went off to Cal, a nickname for the University of California at Berkeley.

Wearing a loose, plum-colored dress that fell waistless from a gathered neckline, Joyce was heavier than the last time I saw her. She appeared soft and womanly, an opinion apparently shared by her partner. He gazed into her face and held her close. Gold lettering on his T-shirt declared, "Dancing is Dandy." She must have brought him to my party, because I didn't recognize him.

When Joyce saw me, she stopped dancing and pulled her young man over to meet me. In my heels, I stood exactly his height. I noticed how soft his eyes looked. And black, so black that the pupils blended in with the iris.

"Mag! Happy birthday! It's been ages. Lord, you're beautiful! So dainty and, unlike me, ugh, slim. But I'm dieting, aren't I, Armando? Mag, this is Armando, Armando Flores. I brought him here because I want you two to dance together."

Grinning, he pulled me into his arms.

"Wait, you idiot! Let her go. Don't mind him, Mag.

He's an absolute idiot, but he's also the most talented male dancer I've ever seen. I just happened to discover him, an original, an untrained primitive, in a dance class I took at Cal. I've tucked him under my wing to guide and nurture him. And I want you to dance with him, Mag, in a ballet I'm doing. Yes, I'm into dancing again. Mostly choreography."

All the time she was talking, this man, this Armando Flores, kept his long-fringed eyes on me. They were cloudy, opaque, centerless. I couldn't see into them, couldn't decide what he was thinking. On the same level as mine, they wouldn't let me look away.

Then, without a word, while Joyce was still talking, his arms settled around me again, held me against his chest, and he led me away in a slow series of spins.

Inches from my face, his dark eyes were pinpointed with lights. And nearly touching my mouth, his smiled, showing perfect teeth. I turned my head away, but against my cheek he whispered soft Spanish words that I couldn't understand. Suddenly, his tongue went into my ear. I stopped dancing.

"What the hell are you doing?" I asked.

"Sticking my tongue in your ear, *pelirrojita*, little red-head. It's such a pretty little ear, like a seashell, a pink flower. I simply couldn't resist."

My face burned but I also felt a delicious excitement.

"How gross. How dare you!"

I pushed against his chest, expecting he would try to hold me there, but, still smiling, he released me.

"Sorry, *pelirrojita*. Don't be mad. I was just playing."

Chapter Five

I don't know whether Joyce saw exactly what Armando had done to me, but she knew something was wrong and hurried over to where we stood facing each other at the edge of the patio.

"What's going on, Mag?" she asked.

"Nothing. Well, I mean, did you see what he did, Joyce?"

I didn't dare look at him. I didn't want to meet those black eyes of his. Beneath my show of anger, he might have sensed my excitement.

"No, I didn't see, but I'm sure it was something outrageous. Honestly, Armando, you've got to curb your impulses when you're around my friends. Especially Mag. She's young and tender and not used to earthy types like you. Remember, I want her, need her, to replace Daphne in our ballet. So say you're sorry."

"*Dispénsame, mi corazón,*" he murmured in the same soft, insinuating Spanish he had crooned against my cheek just before he did what he had done.

"Idiot! Tell her in English, plain, sensible English!"

"Please forgive me. I was only playing."

I glanced sideways in time to catch the gaze as thick and sweet as honey that he poured on her before he turned to me. Obviously, they were lovers!

"That's all right, Joyce," I said. "I knew he was only teasing."

"And you'll be in my ballet, Mag? I submitted it on tape and made the finals in City Ballet's Choreographic Competition. We have to present the ballet to a group of judges at the Company's school. Lord, doesn't it remind you of the time we gave my *Golden Shoes* for the Regional Ballet's Adjudicator?"

"Well, *Golden Shoes* made it to the Festival. Maybe this one will win."

"Who knows? I'll be happy if they give me a little money or an honorable mention. But wouldn't it be great if the Company actually liked it enough to produce it? I think you'll adore it, Mag. I set it on the dance class at Berkeley, but the girl who did the lead, Daphne, took off for Europe."

"Unfortunately," Armando said drily with a faint smile.

Joyce looked at him and away.

"Actually, I'm glad she left, that is, if you'll take the role, Mag, because you're a much better dancer in every way. McMichael said we could rehearse at his studio."

"Well, I'll certainly think about it."

Then I saw Mama bringing Lupe and Eddy out on the patio. I hurried toward them, happy to get away from Armando.

Holding hands tightly, both blinked at the people and the swaying colored lanterns. The pair looked shy and small, like a little brother and sister brought downstairs to say goodnight to the grown-up guests. Then I noticed that Lupe no longer wore her new red dress. She had changed into a dark cotton that made her skin look ashen.

Seeing me, Lupe pushed forward with relief. I hugged her and while her eyes shone sideways at him, I shook Eddy's hand.

"Lupe's told me a lot about you, Eddy, so I feel we're already friends."

"Oh, thank you so much, Maggie. It was great of you to invite us."

He smiled and smiled, almost bowed, overdid his gratitude, it seemed to me. He used a lot of Spanish vowel sounds in his English and I remembered Lupe telling me that his family, like hers, came from Mexico.

"Come and have something to eat," I said, starting toward the buffet table. "Or would you rather dance awhile first?"

"Didn't I tell you, *cariña*? Eddy don't dance."

Lupe's voice turned husky, her grammar lapsed, and her eyes turned anxiously to his smiling face. Only then did I remember her saying that Eddy had given up Catholicism to join some fundamentalist Protestant group which didn't approve of dancing. And Lupe, a talented dancer and company apprentice, loved this man! No wonder her hand pressed the medal hidden under the dark dress. I felt terrible to have brought up what must be a big problem for them.

"Sorry. Oh, I'm sorry. Then do have something to eat."

"Oh, thank you so much, Maggie, but we have to go. Remember, sweetheart, we have a prayer meeting before the fellowship hour. And we don't want to be late, do we?" Eddy said.

I stood teetering on my high heels, troubled by his constant smile. Thank heavens, Paul came over.

"Hey, Lupe, you made it. Hello, I'm Paul Lawrence. Glad to meet you, Eddy. Lupe's a real friend as well as a wonderful dancer."

They shook hands while Joyce, who had followed me across the patio to greet the newcomers, smothered Lupe in a hug. Armando stood silently regarding everybody with his black centerless eyes.

"Lupe!" Joyce cried. "I knew you from clear across the

45

patio. Even with these nearsighted eyes of mine. It's been ages! It was your hair that I recognized first. It's grown back as thick and shiny as before you were sick. But you're as tiny as ever, though much less skinny. And prettier. And I can see why. Who is he, this dark, gorgeous man?"

"Well, this is Eddy. And Eddy, honey, this is an old friend of mine. Joyce used to study with Maggie and me a long time ago at McMichael's."

"But Lupe and Maggie stuck it out to become brilliant dancers. The key was, they had the right body types and talent. I had neither. Finally, I got discouraged and went off to college. But I've come back, Lupe, to try choreography again. Once into dancing, always into dancing. It gets in the blood, you know, Eddy."

I saw Lupe lift her eyes to his face and I tried to signal Joyce to stop talking about dancing, but she didn't understand and her words flowed on and on.

"I brought Armando here especially to meet Maggie. He's a dancer, too, and I want them together in this new Mexican ballet of mine. Her paleness and his darkness. Besides, he may just turn out to be the greatest male dancer since Baryshnikov. If he behaves and pays attention to McMichael's teaching, and works hard, that is."

Armando, blank-faced despite her praise and implied rebuke, extended a hand to Eddy. To my surprise, Eddy stopped smiling and kept his hand at his side while their two pairs of eyes met. Instead of shaking hands, they snarled at each other in Spanish. They clenched their fists, bristled at each other like a pair of vicious dogs.

"Eddy, honey, let's go. We don't want to be late for church."

Lupe's eyes begged and her hands pulled on one of his.

"Please, Eddy, come on."

Finally, he turned abruptly and practically dragged Lupe after him back through the house and out the front door.

"Jesus! What was that all about?" Joyce asked. "I couldn't understand. What did he say to you, Armando?"

"Oh, nothing much. In street Spanish, which they don't teach you at Cal, *mujer*, the bastard questioned my manhood, whether male dancers are real men. He thinks we're all fags."

"Well, all he had to do was ask me," Joyce said.

Blushing, I refused to look at Armando, who stood beside me, thick and warm and full of laughter.

"Come on, Paul, dance with me," I said. But dancing with him was like dancing with a zombie. And when I looked up, the thin veil hid his eyes.

"What's wrong, Paul?"

"Nothing. Hey, nothing's wrong, Maggie. Really. I just get sort of fed up sometimes that everybody automatically thinks a man's gay just because he's a dancer. Some are; some aren't."

"Of course. Come on, let's eat. I haven't had anything much since breakfast."

"Besides, your friend Doug is still over by the food, right?"

But when I looked, he wasn't. My heart did a double beat. Had he left, gone back to Foster City without even saying good-bye?

Then I saw his blond head and red beard circling high above most of the other guests, almost nudging the lanterns and low-sweeping oak limbs. Who did he think he was, dancing with some girl I used to know at Mc-Michael's when he had turned down my invitation?

I edged through the wheeling, stamping couples to where Doug bobbed with a tall girl whose name I couldn't even remember for sure. Libbie, maybe. I tapped Libbie's shoulder.

"Hi, Libbie. Nice to see you again. Sorry to cut in like this, but it seemed the only way to get together with my old high school friend here."

"That's okay, Maggie," Libbie said. "Happy birthday!"

I expected Doug, wanted him, to hold me in dance position, but, without touching me, he started hopping opposite me. I imitated his bobbing little steps.

"I see you finally stopped eating."

"I was hungry. Besides you've seemed pretty occupied all evening with your friend Paul."

"With Paul?"

Now if he had said with Armando, I might have felt a little guilty.

"Paul and I are just friends. Besides, what about Charmaine? You arrived with her on what I thought was our date."

"Listen, Mag. I told you Charmaine needed a ride. What I want to know is, who invited Paul along? And then jumped into the back seat with him?"

"What else could I do when Charmaine grabbed the front seat and then cooed all the way to Foster City about your evenings together? Studying. Studying what, I'd like to know?"

"Engineering, Mag. Engineering."

"I'll bet, with a body like hers!"

We had stopped dancing. And while dancers moved around us, we stood panting, firing off our charges and countercharges.

"Yes, with a body like hers. I told you, Mag, she's an engineering major. That's all we talk about. Engineering. But even after I dropped her off in Foster City, you stayed back there cuddling with Paul."

"Cuddling? I was sitting next to him, that's all."

"Maggie, I saw his arm around you."

"So? He's a good friend. And a dancer. And dancers hug and touch all the time. It doesn't mean anything. Besides, I saw you kissing Charmaine there on her front porch."

"I did not kiss Charmaine."

"Okay. She kissed you. What's the difference?"

"Maggie! We're getting nowhere. And, after finals, I'm dead tired. So I guess I'll just say good night."

He left me, dodged among the dancers, headed for the living room. I followed him.

"And go back to Foster City, I suppose, where you intended to end up all along?"

He didn't answer, just went through the open glass doors, ducking a little to avoid hitting his head, a habit his six-feet-four-inches often made necessary.

Inside, Doug shook hands with my parents. Then they all glanced toward me in the doorway. Doug lifted his hand in a stiff unsmiling salute and disappeared into the entrance hall. Should I go after him? But what was the use?

I returned to the patio and listened for the roar of Doug's car or, perhaps, for the sound of his horn that long ago he used to toot twice in farewell. But the disco was too loud. What a terrible night! First, no apprenticeship. Now, no Doug!

Well, I would show him. I would dance with every man here! But on my way back to the party, I tripped on my long green skirt, stumbled on the steps, and would have fallen except for an arm that caught me around the waist. It was Armando's arm.

Chapter Six

In bed the next morning I was dimly aware of my canary cheeping and trying some tentative warbles inside his covered cage. But it was my father's voice outside my room that awoke me. Why hadn't he gone off to make his early hospital calls? Already, sunlight pressed through the white drapes filling my whole bedroom with a warm milkiness.

"If she'd been wearing sensible shoes, not those damned ankle breakers . . ." my father rumbled. He was talking to Mama, of course, but her replies, if any, were inaudible.

"Fortunately, that Mexican kid caught her, so I don't think there's any damage. But, dammit, Elizabeth, she's worn out from this ballet. She's got to be sensible. She's got to wear sensible shoes. She's got to rest—only do enough dancing to stay limber—for at least a month."

A month? I reared up on my elbows. What about my career? What career? But, at least, there was Joyce's ballet with "that Mexican kid." I was scared to dance with Armando but, at the same time, I longed to. And if I had to take it easy for a whole month . . . Carefully, carefully, I stretched my left leg, pointed my left foot, flexed it. Not even a twinge!

"And, by the way," my father boomed out in the hall, "who was that kid anyway? The one who carried her in.

51

You remember, the short dark Mexican boy. Very muscular. Not a new boyfriend, I hope."

In my room I sank back on my pillow, brushed aside the tangled mass of my hair, pulled up the lacy strap that had slid off my shoulder. No, Father, Armando Flores is not my boyfriend. He's Joyce's, I think. So why do I let his eyes fascinate me when he's hers and I love Doug? Or did. Oh, forget Doug!

"Because I didn't like the way that boy was bound and determined to carry her into her bedroom last night. I tried to pry her out of his arms, but he held on, so all I could do was go along with them. And after he laid her on the bed, he hung around while I examined her ankle."

Yes, I remembered Armando in his gold-logoed T-shirt in the lamplight at the foot of my bed last night. His arms, hugging the brass rails, ballooned with muscles. Most of the time his eyes had watched mine, but sometimes he followed my father's cool, skilled fingers probing my foot, ankle, and Achilles tendon. And once, only once, some warmer, thicker fingers sent a shiver from my ankle up my leg, through my entire body. Or did I only imagine that warmer touch?

Now my father's knock shook my hollow plywood door.

"Are you awake, Maggie?"

"Now I am."

"Good. I want to talk to you before I leave."

I huddled farther down in bed, pulled the top sheet over my lacy nightgown. Help me to be calm! He came in, frowning, his green eyes, smaller than mine but the same color, peering down at me.

"You're looking thin, Maggie. Too pale. Your skin's almost translucent. You look exhausted, practically anorexic. As usual, you're overdoing the damned dancing. How's the ankle this morning?"

His cool hand pulled back the sheet to feel along my left ankle.

"Any pain?"

I shook my head.

"Good. I don't feel any swelling either. You're lucky. Just too damned much dancing. That's all that's wrong. You've got to rest."

"Yes, Father."

"Don't 'Yes, Father' me, Maggie. I mean it. No classes. No rehearsals. Nothing more than a few stretching exercises for at least a month."

"Yes, Father."

A long time ago I used to call him Papa. Papa, Mama, and Mags. When did I switch to Father?

"Dammit, Maggie. Don't just say yes. When are you supposed to go back to the City to start working with the company? When does your apprenticeship start?"

I saw his broad face flushing with temper—a temper I had inherited from him. I didn't dare look at Mama who had just come in. I knew my answer would come out nearly swallowed and all shaky. It did.

"I didn't—didn't get one."

"You didn't get an apprenticeship."

It wasn't a question—he said it quietly. He merely repeated what I had said.

I shook my head and waited for an explosion of I-told-you-so's. But my confession seemed to have shaken him. Had he finally accepted my dancing? Come to believe in my talent after all these years?

"I'm sorry, Mags."

I looked up and saw Mama routinely uncovering the canary cage as she did every morning.

"Me too, baby, me too. How awful. How unfair. After all your hard work."

I felt tears starting. I mean, I had been ready to defy especially my father, to shout back, to demand the right to live my own life. But, suddenly, the wall between us seemed to have crumbled and so did my will to hold back my sobs.

"Everything's ended, finished."

My father sat down on the edge of the bed, stroked my head, which I rolled back and forth on the pillow.

"Now, Mags, calm down. Lie still. Elizabeth, get her that box of Kleenex off her dresser. You don't have to make plans today, Mags. Besides, it's probably too late now to get into a four-year college next fall, but you could inquire up at the junior college."

"What?"

I sat up again.

"I don't believe this! College! You still are trying to run my life, after all!"

I felt tricked into letting down my guard, felt the wall rise between us again.

"I don't want to go to college, Father. That's the last place I want to go. I want to dance."

"Calm down, Maggie. I'm not asking you to give up dancing. You could dance in college. I'm only saying that this summer, during the remainder of June and most of July, you should rest. But while you're resting, you can think about your future, look at your options. Because, by September . . ."

"By September, what?"

I heard my mother clicking her tongue, asking, "Can't this wait, Will, until she's calmer?"

"No. I didn't mean to bring it up now, but since it has come up, we might as well discuss it. By September, Maggie, I think you should either be going to college or supporting yourself. And if you can't get a job dancing and don't want to go to college, you'll have to find some kind of work to pay for your lessons and to support yourself."

I rubbed at my eyes with the wet Kleenex balled up in my hand and pulled another from the box.

"Fine. I'll do that. I'll apply at Swensen's and at Jack-in-the-Box. I don't mind working. But what I don't understand, what I've never understood, is why you'll pay to send me to college but won't pay for my ballet lessons."

"Because, Maggie, college will prepare you to earn your own living. And ballet lessons won't, unless you're fantastically talented. Which, apparently, you aren't or your great school in the City would have given you an apprenticeship."

"But it was politics, Father. It was that fag Randall wanting only male apprentices."

"Maggie, if the directors had believed in you enough . . ."

"They do, or most of them do. It's just this stupid new policy. But even if I had received an apprenticeship, I couldn't have lived on the stipend the ballet company pays. Would you still have cut off my allowance?"

"That's different. If you had received an apprenticeship, I would probably have continued your allowance. I would consider an apprenticeship a pretty good indication that you have enough talent to succeed as a professional dancer. But you didn't receive one."

"No."

"So unless something else turns up before September . . ."

The sentence hung unfinished while he looked at his watch.

"Anyway, now I have to get over to the hospital. And, Maggie, I am sorry you didn't get your apprenticeship. Believe me, I really am."

He leaned to kiss my forehead, but I twisted away.

"Well, see you later, Elizabeth," he said, sighing. "Try to calm her down."

After my father left, Mama sighed too.

"I thought all that was over and finished. Besides, I was sure you would get an apprenticeship. Well, maybe the San Francisco Ballet will take you. Or maybe you could go to Los Angeles."

I lay back on my pillow.

"Maybe. It's easier with your own company though, I think, because you're known. But I'll try anything, anywhere."

Then out in the hall the phone rang and I ran to answer it. Maybe it was Doug.

It wasn't. It was Joyce.

"Mag, how's the ankle?"

"Fine."

"Why do you sound so dejected then?"

"Well, I just went through another round of the same old battle with my father. I know the script by heart. Besides which, I didn't get an apprenticeship."

"I know. Your friend Paul told me last night. It's criminal, Mag! It really is. And I suppose that's what precipitated the battle with dear old Dad?"

"Yes."

"Mag, I have the solution to all your problems! Remember the ballet I mentioned? Well, the Competition's the first Sunday in August and the judges will be . . ."

"Sunday?"

"Yes, because of summer session classes the rest of the week. I wanted to discuss all this with you last night but then you fell. And the last I saw of you was your dad and Armando carrying you off into your bedroom."

Remembering the warmth of Armando's arm through

the thin silk of my dress and his jaw resting briefly against my cheek, I felt guilty. But I didn't try to defend myself. After all I had done nothing, been completely passive.

"Well, Mag, if you do dance in my ballet, and you've got to, the company directors, who are judging the Competition, would get to see you in performance. And they would be sure to give you your apprenticeship. Which would assure Dad that you have an abundance of talent. There, I've solved all your problems."

"Nearly all."

I didn't mention Doug.

"So how about it, can you be at McMichael's in an hour to begin rehearsing? We have to use the studio early before he starts teaching."

"Okay, I'll be there."

"You're sure your ankle's okay?"

"Positive."

"Good. And, Mag, your friend Paul and I got to talking outside your room last night. He won't have much time to rehearse because of his apprenticeship, but he agreed to do an easy role in my ballet. In fact, my mother and I put him up last night so he could be at the rehearsal this morning."

"That was nice of you."

"And the main reason he agreed to be in the ballet was because you're in it. From what he said, I thought you wouldn't mind working with him either."

"Of course not. But I don't understand. What did he say about us? I mean, he's often my partner, but we're only friends."

"Are you sure, Mag?"

"Positive. Why?"

"Well, something is certainly bothering him. And I

think it's you. For one thing, he seemed definitely annoyed not to have been the one to save you last night. I must admit, I was a little annoyed myself. Though, by this time, I've learned to accept Armando for what he is. At least, I hope so."

"I'm awfully sorry, Joyce."

"Relax, Mag. It wasn't your fault. It's just Armando. Incidently, it would be convenient, on his way, you know, for him to pick you up. He lives in Sunnyvale."

"No. Oh, no. I can borrow Mama's car."

I spoke too quickly, but Joyce sounded relieved.

"It's probably just as well. For one thing, he drives a motorcycle. And I don't imagine your dad, being a doctor, or your mom either, would want their precious little daughter riding tandem on a black Yamaha. I can see you now, clutching Armando's waist, your hair whipping out behind like a red warning flag. Well, see you in an hour, Mag."

When I started out the kitchen door, Mama widened her eyes at me.

"Your father said, 'No dancing.' "

"He just said not to overdo, Mama. That's all."

Chapter Seven

An hour later I knocked at McMichael's locked studio. The door and windows were made of green glass and turned the foyer into an aquarium, the rubber tree into a tall floating sea plant.

Joyce came to let me in just as Paul entered the waiting room. And where was Armando? I forced myself to keep from looking into the studio or toward the hall that led to the dressing rooms. Our voices and footsteps rang in the emptiness and silence.

Paul and I hugged; then I finally had to see who was in the classroom. Vacant. Joyce bit her thumbnail.

"Mag, if you're looking for Armando, he hasn't shown up yet. He's always late. Maybe by the time you've changed and warmed up he'll be here."

"Oh, I wasn't looking for Armando, Joyce. Where are the others? The kids from Berkeley?"

"I'll be working with just you and Paul today. And Armando, if he shows up. The Berkeley kids won't rehearse with us until later; and then, only those who haven't left for the summer. I'll have to fill in with some of McMichael's older students. Go get dressed now."

When I returned in tights and leotard, she had not switched on the electricity. The studio was lit only by shadowy green sunlight that filtered through eucalyptus trees and entered the high transoms that rimmed three sides of the classroom. To my surprise, a carved wooden drum wobbled at the center of the floor. The hide of some animal—sheep, deer, ocelot—was stretched across the top. Joyce laughed at my baffled look.

"Well, what did you expect, Mag? A concert grand? It's an Indian ballet, Mexican Indian, so, of course, this drum is going to be our accompaniment, with an occasional bit of flute music. I'll tape the whole thing and only pretend to beat the drum."

I didn't say anything, just started to warm up, but my doubt about her ballet must have shown.

"Don't worry, Mag. You'll love it when you get used to it."

"But I hardly look Indian. Neither does Paul."

"Of course not. The paler the better. You and Paul are pale, washed-out, gringo tourists, slumming through a *zócalo*, a plaza deep in the heart of Mexico on a market day. White-trousered or -skirted Indians, depending on their sex, squat half asleep behind pyramids of plums and cactus fruit, behind raw, red pottery and crudely blown glass. None of these will really be there; they'll be merely suggested with gestures. Indians wander in and stagger out of the *pulquería*, doze under big hats. Get the picture? Stereotyped Mexican market scene. Okay? And that's the backdrop—a Mexican plaza projected from a slide."

Still unconvinced, I switched from *pliés* to *tendus*. Paul leaned on the *barre*, watching me. Joyce in slacks and black ballet slippers paced back and forth, her hands pantomiming furiously.

"You come along, flirting your full-skirted green dress, Mag, like the one you wore to your party. In fact, how about using that one? And you're carrying a wide-brimmed hat with a green velvet band."

"Mama has a white straw picture hat she wore to a garden wedding once."

"Great. Ask her if we can borrow it. In the beginning of the ballet you're adventurous, laughing, arm-in-arm with reluctant Paul who detests Mexico. The plumbing's crude, the electricity's uncertain, the water's polluted. Why couldn't you have vacationed at some reasonable, civilized place like Waikiki or the Bahamas? Get over there, Paul. Come on, Mag, take his arm. Let's see it."

"But do we do all this just to drum beats and flute?" I asked, hooking an arm through one of Paul's, hoping this wasn't as strange and amateurish as it sounded. After all, Joyce was presenting it to judges who would be considering not only her ballet, but me again, maybe for an apprenticeship.

"No, Mag, not all of it's to drum and flute. At the end come a couple of blasts on a conch shell that I borrowed from a university collection. And this first part is without any music."

"It all seems pretty strange."

"As we work through it, you'll get the picture. I'm trying to depict a mood I felt about Mexico in some of the writings of D. H. Lawrence. In one of his short stories, a North American woman lets herself be captured and sacrificed by an ancient Indian tribe. The main source is Lawrence's novel, *Quetzalcoatl* or *The Plumed Serpent*, which is the name of an ancient Mexican god. I call the ballet *The Plumed Serpent*, too."

I glanced at Paul to see what he thought of all this. He smiled reassuringly.

"Hey, it sounds great to me, Joyce!"

"Good. Okay, kids, now bounce downstage and skip through a chain of twisting *glissades*. Da-da! Da-da! Da-da! End with a skirt-whipping spin on one *pointe*, a single

61

fouetté. Light. Carefree. Girlish. Coy. You know you're pretty, Mag. You're performing, showing-off for the sluggish Indians, the backward savages. The natives."

She clapped out a beat. I skimmed the *glissades*, whirled into the *fouetté*.

"Catch her, Paul, at the apex of the turn. Lift her from the waist, stretch her high above your head."

Joyce nodded.

"That's it. Catch her in midair. Sort of pick her off the wind like a particle of thistledown. Now let her slide down your body, hook her around; now pivot in a dream-like waltz; hold her away from you. Look at her as if you think she's the loveliest, most enchanting girl you ever saw. Even though she dragged you down to this awful Mexico."

We waltzed, smiling into each other's faces, but I was wondering what Armando's role could be in this weird ballet.

Then, just outside the ballet school, a motorcycle came rumbling. It snorted and coughed into silence.

"Finally!" Joyce said.

She hurried to the back door which opened directly from the classroom into a dry neglected garden ringed by eucalyptus trees. Gray-green clumps of chrysanthemums struggled out of eucalyptus debris and stony baked mud. A group of ancient rose bushes grew more thorns than blossoms.

Through the garden and into the doorway sauntered Armando. He paused, silhouetted against the shimmering late June heat. He kissed Joyce, then hugged her with an arm that was bare to the sleeve of his black T-shirt. The other arm hugged a shining black motorcycle helmet. Joyce laughed self-consciously. Joyce, self-conscious?

"Our Aztec god, our modern day Huitzilopochtli has arrived appropriately on his motorcycle."

"Wow, that's a mouthful! I thought the god was called Quetzal–something," I said, partly to smooth over Joyce's sudden, unusual shyness and partly because I knew nothing about Mexican mythology.

"One of the gods was called Quetzalcoatl or The Plumed Serpent. He was a benign, blond god, worshipped by most of the ancient cultures of central Mexico. The Aztecs were expecting his return when Cortez turned up."

"Then who's the other one?"

"Huitzilopochtli. He was the powerful sun god who apparently was worshipped only by the Aztecs. In order to keep him strong and happy, the Indians sacrificed to him, cut out the hearts of their captives. Armando dances Huitzilopochtli."

She freed herself from his hug.

"At least he will, if he can get here on time. Where have you been, Armando? Maggie and Paul are almost through the prologue."

Smiling, Armando stowed his helmet in her arms and then stalked across the studio on thick, muscular legs forced into tight jeans. He stopped close to where I stood beside Paul.

"Here you are, *pelirrojita*!"

Blushing under his steady gaze, I stepped backward and landed on one of Paul's feet.

"Oh, sorry. I'm sorry, Paul."

To make things worse, Joyce was right there. She hooked an arm through one of Armando's.

"All right, lover-boy. We'll continue with the prologue while you go change and warm up."

"But I ain't changing, *mujer*. And I ain't warming up."

He grinned at her, trying to bug her, I could tell, with his ungrammatical English.

"Listen, Armando, if you want to be in my ballet, if you want to become a dancer, if you want to be seen by the people at City Ballet . . ."

"Okay, okay. I get the picture. Besides, I was only playing."

He left and the three of us looked after him. Joyce turned her back to Paul and me.

"Shit! But he's so damned talented. Come on, where were we? Yes, the silly little waltz in the middle of the *zócalo* under the high Aztec sun."

We went on with the waltz, but listlessly, hardly thinking about what we were doing, because the room was growing sultry and our minds were on Armando. At least mine was. And the other two seemed equally distracted.

When Armando returned, he still wore his black T-shirt, but had stripped down to black tights. They clung to his muscular thighs and haunches as if he were naked. In fact, naked he might have looked less masculine. For the tights and his athletic supporter created a bulge that resembled a large redwood burl.

"Okay, kids," Joyce said, "I'll talk through the next part while Armando warms up."

"Do I have to?"

She shot him a look that sent him to the *barre* in an exaggerated hurry.

"Okay. Okay. I'll warm up. Anything you say, *mujer!*"

She turned her back on him.

"All right, Paul, Maggie, while you're waltzing, drum beats begin."

Joyce kicked off her ballet shoes and began walking, leaning forward, gradually sinking into a heavy rhythm.

"I want you to get this exactly right. It's not as easy as it looks. One, two. One, two. Down, down. Down, down."

Watching Joyce begin the traditional circle dance, listening to her voice that was almost chanting, I began to feel her ballet, to catch its spirit, to experience an almost hypnotic spell.

"After a while an Indian asks Mag to dance."

"And I," declared Armando, leaping in front of me, "am that Indian!"

Joyce waved him toward the *barre*.

"Get back over there. You haven't warmed up enough. I'll call you when I need you."

"Ah, but you always need me, *mi corazón*."

The soft lull of his voice made me shiver. Maybe Joyce too. But she frowned, then laughed.

"You're impossible, Armando. Oh, all right. All right. Only don't blame me if you pull a muscle."

"Never!"

Grabbing me into dancing position, he whirled me across the room in an astonishing, exaggerated polka.

"Armando, let her go! If you're going to be a dancer, you've got to learn self-discipline."

But Armando rocked me on and on, his black eyes challenging me to participate in something more, I felt sure, than a polka or an ancient circle dance. Joyce grew shrill. Finally, she walked out of the room. I pushed him away.

"Now look what you've done, Armando. Poor Joyce. I'll go talk to her."

"No, *chiquita*, you stay here. I'll go. I know just how to bring her round."

After he left, Paul and I avoided looking at each other. We walked through the waltz several more times, pan-

65

tomiming the lift with our hands, not dancing full-out because we were both tired.

Later when Joyce and Armando returned, arms festooned around each other's waists, she wore a little smile. But when she wasn't looking, he shut one eye at me in a slow, heavy wink.

Chapter Eight

That afternoon Paul returned to San Francisco where he was now an apprentice. For him, graduation really did mean a beginning.

For Joyce and me, the rest of June and first two weeks of July, except for the three-day Fourth of July weekend, were spent working. My ankle and tendon gave me no trouble. Usually we practiced alone because most days, for various reasons, Armando skipped rehearsals. But every morning Joyce and I worked on her ballet. For in spite of my ten years of ballet training, or maybe because of them, the bent-kneed Indian tread, that looked so easy came hard.

"It's not upbeat like ballet, Mag. No wind lifts you," she said one morning.

How did she know about my summer wind? I had never mentioned it to her. I had told Lupe, of course, because no matter how silly something sounded, I knew Lupe wouldn't laugh.

"It's downbeat, Mag, the earth is dragging on you, pulling you down to its source, making you part of it."

I leaned forward and slid my feet along.

"That's better. In this ballet of mine you begin as a pale *gringa*, but gradually the Indian . . . that damned Armando. I'll just bet he had to drive his mother to the clinic this morning! On his motorcycle? Sure he did! Anyway, little by little with his hand heavy on your wrist, like this, he drags you into the deep slow rhythm."

She pressed her hand on my wrist.

"Down, Mag. Think heavy. That's it. That's better. And tomorrow, he'd better be here. Armando, that is. We need him for the final parts of the ballet, when he finally winds you into the very center, the core of the moving spiral."

But the next morning, while Joyce and I were warming up, the telephone rang hollowly in the deserted building. The sound reminded me of a favorite fairytale that Papa, as I called him then, used to read to me when I was little. In the story, although a village had sunk to the bottom of the sea, its church bells continued to ring.

Joyce ran to the foyer to answer the phone. At first she kept her voice too low for me to hear, but soon she was shouting.

"That's bullshit, Armando. You must think I'm some sort of imbecile, or dizzy with love, to believe an excuse like that. The Competition is the first Sunday in August. That gives us barely two weeks. So you have twenty minutes to get down here or you're out of my ballet! Out of my life!"

Crash. The receiver went back to its cradle. When I came into the foyer, Joyce sat at the desk. She stared straight across the waiting room, through the green-tinted glass, and through the midmorning traffic. Her stare stubbed up against the stucco box that housed the doughnut shop across the street.

"Damn him!"

Her voice trembled, but not her jaw, not that square jaw of hers.

"Let's break for doughnuts, Mag. Let's pig-out."

"What about your diet?"

68

She sniffed.

"Do you know what his excuse was this time? Relatives arrived from Mexico and he's having to help entertain them. At ten o'clock in the morning? Unless he's still entertaining them from last night. Maybe a pretty second cousin. Or noncousin. Well, he'd better get over here fast!"

I had never seen her so out of control. Lupe, yes, with her anorexia, her superstitious dependence on her St. Christopher, and now her blind love for Eddy. And, of course, me! Temperamental, excitable me. Just ask my father! But Joyce was always level-headed, always wise, always reasonable.

"But how can we do the ballet without him?"

"We can't. Of course, we can't do *Serpent* without him. And I can't do without him either. If he doesn't show up soon, I'll die. Or I'll go up to Sunnyvale and personally cut out his heart."

Then my wise, reasonable friend put her head down on the desk and cried.

"Take it easy, Joyce."

"I'm an idiot, Mag. I've known what he was from the beginning—since he started playing around with Daphne before she left my ballet. So why can't I just see him as a very talented dancer? Or why can't I just enjoy him as he enjoys me and a dozen other women with no pretense of love? But I go crazy when I see him touching, or even think of him touching, another girl. Daphne, for one. Even you, Mag!"

I moved away from her. And to think I had been stupid enough to complain to her the other night when he stuck his tongue in my ear.

"Well, I know how you feel, Joyce. Come on. Let's go get some doughnuts. Maybe things aren't as bad as you think."

She laughed deep in her chest like an opera singer.

"Oh, they're as bad, Mag. Worse, probably. Entertaining relatives! Shit! You'd think he would take the trouble to invent something more plausible. Or maybe he doesn't care, doesn't want me to believe him. Wants to torment me."

"Oh, he's not like that, Joyce."

"I know. He's not mean. And he's honest. Too honest."

Pulling jeans and sweat shirts over our practice clothes, we crossed the street while the cars were halted by traffic lights. When I opened the door to the doughnut shop the delicious sugary fragrance carried me back to the days when Joyce and I used to reward ourselves after class. We would sit on these doll-sized metal chairs around one of the little round tables with Lupe. On the verge of anorexia then, she used to insist that she wanted only a glass of water while Joyce and I gobbled doughnuts.

Today after choosing my old favorite, a long sugared cylinder oozing raspberry jelly, I sat down across from Joyce at a window table. She had already finished one of her spiraled cinnamon rolls.

Her face looked composed, resigned, lifeless really. But behind it, if she were like me when I thought about Doug or my lost apprenticeship, her thoughts and feelings must be all knotted and tangled with self-doubt and jealousy.

"What will you do if he doesn't show up, Joyce?"

"There are other dancers, other fish in the sea."

"You don't believe that."

"No, but it's true. There are other men."

"Not for me. For me, there's only Doug. And for Lupe, I'm sure, there's only Eddy."

When I looked out the window, there he was, Eddy, passing inches away from us on the other side of the window. Impulsively, I rapped on the pane. He looked at me, then away again.

70

"He doesn't recognize you, Mag. But, good heavens, Lupe's with him. Isn't she supposed to be in San Francisco?"

We hadn't seen her at first because she was hidden by Eddy. Now she dropped back a step. Smiling and waving at us, she tugged on Eddy's arm. She gestured toward the door of the doughnut shop. Eddy finally smiled at us but he shook his head at her and pointed down the street. Lupe's mouth crumpled. I saw a flash of tears along the lower rims of her eyes. But she waved good-bye and trotted after him.

"Poor Lupe," Joyce said. "That cold, cold smile of his. They must be going to church. It's in a storefront a couple of blocks from here, I think."

Watching Lupe trail after Eddy, I felt like crying.

"She should be in San Francisco, the same as Paul. The company's rehearsing for the summer repertory performances. And there she is, down here, tagging after old Smiley. But at least, he loves her."

"Maybe, in his own way. Or maybe he loves the girl he thinks she is or wants her to become. Maybe that's better than not being loved at all."

One of her fingers traced spirals in the sugar on her fluted paper plate. She licked the sweetness from her finger and then chewed her thumbnail.

Just then above the hum of traffic came the thunder of a motorcycle. I saw it in midair, its twin mirrors shining, its silver motor and twin pipes gleaming. Mounted on its black leather saddle was a rider in black leather armor.

"My God, it's Armando," Joyce cried. "He must have jumped the curb. He rides that thing like a bucking bronco or a jousting knight. Someday the crazy fool will kill himself."

71

Although she spoke of death, life poured back into her body and voice. She sprang out of her seat, accidentally overturning her chair, and rushed to the door.

"Go on and finish your doughnut, Mag. I'll see you in a little while."

Through the window I watched Joyce teeter on the curb, impatient for the train of cars to make a path for her. Finally she plunged in anyway, wading and dodging through the halting, honking traffic. Dear God, she would be killed! But she arrived alive on the other side where Armando's arms went around her. Making all her trials worthwhile? Well, she was in his arms, anyway. And Lupe was with Eddy. Only I, I had nothing, nobody.

Leaving the table, I went to the public telephone near the door and quickly dialed Doug's house. While I counted the rings—one, two, three—I noticed that the phone was painted white with a sprinkling of fat, red, strawberry-shaped hearts. How silly. But how appropriate this morning.

Doug's mother answered. After nearly three years I still recognized her careful English with its slight Swedish accent.

"Oh, yes, Maggie. How are you? No, Douglas is at work. He has a summer job, you know. Was it something special? Oh, well then, I'll just tell him you called."

Click. My connection to Doug was broken again. And maybe she was glad. She was a widow. Doug, Douglas was her only child. Nothing special, I had assured her. No, nothing, just my life. "Oh, don't dramatize, Maggie!" I could hear my father saying.

When I crossed back to the ballet school, Joyce was leaving with Armando. She waved happily.

"We're going to Santa Cruz, to the beach. On the motorcycle—would you believe?"

"What about rehearsal?" I asked.

"Tomorrow," she said.

"*Mañana*," he said. His white teeth flashed signals, but this time he didn't wink.

That night after dinner, Doug returned my call.

"Hi, Mag, I was really happy you phoned. But surprised."

"Surprised?"

I eyed my parents bent over supper at the kitchen table.

"Wait a minute. It's too noisy in here. Hang it up for me, will you, Mama?"

In their bedroom, I picked up the receiver.

"Here I am again, Doug. Where were we?"

"You were surprised that I was surprised."

"Yes."

"Well, I'll tell you why. All that night, during the drive down from San Francisco and during your party I got the distinct impression that you didn't have time for me, that you were as involved in ballet—not to mention with that blond ballet dancer—as you were in high school. No, Mag, it's true. I wish it weren't."

"What's really true is that you were so wrapped up in Charmaine that you hardly noticed me. To get you even to dance with me, I had to cut in on Libbie. And then you up and left in the middle of the party. To head right back to Charmaine, I'm sure."

"No, Mag. I went home to bed. Remember, I was exhausted from a week of finals."

"And never set eyes on her again, I suppose you're going to tell me next."

"You gave me no reason not to see her, Mag. So we've been going out some."

"Oh, well, then, you probably have a date with her right now, so don't let me hold you up one single second longer!"

I slammed down the receiver, threw myself on my parents' bed, and sobbed against their satin bedspread.

Chapter Nine

During the next two weeks, rehearsing Joyce's *Plumed Serpent* helped keep my mind off Doug. And, most of the time, off Armando too, except, of course, as a dancing partner.

To my surprise, he now showed up nearly every day. If he wasn't there exactly at eight, at least he arrived soon enough each morning to tramp through the slow spiraling dance with me and a few of McMichael's students-turned-Indians and then to twist me through a violent *pas de deux*.

Joyce had redone the variation for me, making it so difficult, so dangerous that I had to concentrate totally on what we were doing. So instead of noticing Armando, the man, I was thankful just for his powerful arms and quick, skillful strength that safely lifted and supported me in those high one-armed thrusts and sudden terrifying dives.

"Relax, Mag," Joyce said one morning. "He won't drop you. The *pas de deux* was simpler in Berkeley, but not that different. Armando has done it dozens of times."

"Sure, *pelirrojita*, like she says, you got to trust me."

Even when we finished rehearsing he seemed to be on his best behavior. He no longer teased or taunted or whatever he did at first with those winks and sexy looks and, for God's sake, his tongue in my ear. No, now, before heading for the dressing room he would give Joyce's waist a lingering squeeze, her neck a nuzzling kiss, or her behind a flip with his rolled-up towel. Then he would laugh and amble off, muttering to himself in Spanish.

So it seemed that whatever she had said to him was working for her. Until the Thursday before the Competition. On that Thursday, when she went off to the waiting room to phone San Francisco to confirm rehearsal space, I remained in the classroom to stretch. The students had retired to the dressing rooms and so had Armando. At least I thought so. But suddenly he was there, behind me as I stood with my right foot turned out, my left resting on the *barre*. He looped one arm around my waist and slid the other along my left leg.

"Now at last, a moment alone with you," he whispered, imitating a French accent, laughing close to my ear. I ducked my head to avoid a repetition of his tongue-in-the-ear trick.

"Get away, Armando."

"Ah, but *pelirrojita*, see in the mirror how good we look together."

Out of the corner of one eye I did notice our reflections: mine, slim and pale; his, thick and dark, but I refused to look directly at our images.

"Go away."

"No. We are too beautiful together. You all milky white with hair like fire and me dark, dark with love for you."

"You don't love me!"

"Well, not like you mean, but we could have fun."

"No. Stop it. Besides Joyce is my good friend."

I swung a shoulder to push him away. He didn't insist. He shrugged and moved away.

"*Mi pobre*, my poor pretty little redhead. Think what you're missing. With me, love is like dancing. So much

76

fun. But you *gringas*—all of you—take love too seriously."

On Friday we went to San Francisco to patch together the whole ballet for the Competition on Sunday. And patch was exactly what we had to do.

In the morning, Joyce drove me up to the City and parked in the lot across the street from City Ballet School. I hadn't been there since driving away in Doug's little orange car.

Joyce and I were climbing out of her mother's old Chevy and collecting our ballet gear from the trunk when Armando bounded into the parking lot on his Yamaha. He leaped off and crossed the street ahead of us. Nervously, I looked at the double glass doors of the ballet school. Was Randall inside? I wasn't up to his haughty stare this morning. But Paul welcomed us at the door.

He gave me a squeeze, hugged Joyce, and shook hands with Armando.

"Hey, Maggie, I've really missed you! Martina is upstairs teaching, but she said to tell you we'll have to use the basement room."

"But it's got a concrete floor. It's only used for meetings. It's really murder on feet and legs, not to mention backs."

"I know, but the summer classes are using all the other studios."

We followed Paul to the cold whitewashed room which, except for the ballet *barres* that rimmed it, was more like a giant freezer than a rehearsal room. It reminded me of the school auditorium where long ago I had danced a demonstration—the Sugarplum Fairy variation—with Randall doing a condescending narration.

Now, after changing into practice clothes and layering our legs and bodies with woolen sweaters and coarse tights, we set to work on my waltz with Paul. When the dancers arrived from Berkeley, Joyce used them to fill out the winding spiral of kids from McMichael's school. A mother with a minibus had driven them to San Francisco. After a while, the concrete floor began to bother some of the kids.

"Listen, everybody," Joyce said. "Just mark it. This damned floor! For heaven's sake, don't hurt yourselves. We need all of you. We don't have any understudies. Not even for Mag's role."

"Maybe we could get Lupe," I said.

"Well, Lupe's sort of preoccupied these days," Paul said. "She's missed several rehearsals. Calls in and says she's sick. She's out today. I'm afraid she may lose her apprenticeship."

I remembered Lupe trailing after Eddy outside the doughnut shop last week when she should have been up here rehearsing.

"Poor Lupe," Joyce said, "but she wouldn't be right for your role anyway, Mag. She's too Indian looking. What we need is another pale *gringa*."

"I know just the girl. Kathy," I said. "She's blond, a good dancer, and a fairly quick study when she concentrates."

Joyce asked all sorts of questions about her technique and physical appearance.

"Oh, forget them boring details, *mujer*. Is she pretty or not?"

Through this, I noticed Paul brooding, rubbing the toes of his shoes in a nearly empty box of rosin.

"She's not pretty at all," he blurted finally, surprising me because he was usually so mild. "She's just your ordinary, anemic *corps de ballet* type. Besides, she doesn't come around here much after not getting an apprenticeship."

"Well, let's get hold of her anyway," Joyce said. "I'd feel much happier if we had somebody covering Mag's role. Try to call her, will you, Mag?"

From the office I telephoned Kathy, but she wasn't at the apartment she shared with Lupe and a young *corps* member named Shirley.

"May I talk to Lupe then, Shirley?"

"She's not here either."

"I thought Lupe was home sick."

"Listen, who is this?"

"It's Maggie. Maggie Adams."

"Oh, hi, Maggie. I thought this might be somebody from the company, checking up on Lupe, because of her apprenticeship, you know. She didn't come back last night. But you can get hold of Kathy at the San Francisco Ballet School. She's taking classes there this summer."

I phoned Kathy at the school and she agreed to come.

She arrived early in the afternoon, but I guess I was too busy treading the inward spiral with Armando to notice her at first. When the pressure of his hand lightened on my wrist, however, I looked up to find him staring toward the doorway.

"So that's Kathy! Sure doesn't fit Paul's description."

He went to greet her.

"Get back there in the circle, lover boy," Joyce called.

"But I simply want to welcome her. *Muy bienvenida, blanquita.*"

Joyce and I joined them at the door. While I made the introductions, Kathy looked across the room at Paul who was fidgeting with the elastic of one shoe.

"Do I get to dance with Paul?" Kathy asked.

"You get to dance with me, *blanquita*. And I with you."

Kathy's pale eyes glanced at him and away. I saw Joyce's jaw tighten.

"You get to work behind Maggie. And you need to pay attention and learn the tread. It's not as easy as it looks."

"I'll be happy to show her," Armando said.

He fell back a step to stamp in place beside Kathy instead of me. Ridiculously, I felt deserted and jealous. And I didn't have to imagine Joyce's feelings!

"Armando! Don't be such a damned fool. Get back there and partner Maggie. Kathy's only covering for her."

"And, therefore, needs all the help I can give her, right, *mujer*?"

Armando's eyes lighted with laughter and darted from Kathy to me; then to Joyce who suddenly stamped her foot on the hard concrete.

"Shit!"

Her eyes flashed with tears. "That's it. End of rehearsal. End of ballet. I'll withdraw it from the Competition. It's not worth all this hassle."

Kathy looked startled. Armando regarded Joyce with maybe a shadow of a smile. I hurried to her. So did Paul. I put my arms around her.

"Armando's only teasing."

"Hey, he doesn't mean any harm. It's a good ballet. A great ballet. You're bound to win with it, Joyce."

"Sure you are," I added. "You're just tired now. Why don't we call it a day and come back tomorrow? The dress rehearsal will go just fine. You'll see."

Chapter Ten

The dress rehearsal Saturday morning did go fairly well. We all turned up rested, Joyce and I from the Peninsula in her mother's Chevy, which, of course, was too tame and was scheduled to arrive too early for Armando. But from the cellar studio we soon heard his Yamaha surge down the street in front of the ballet school.

"Only half an hour late," Joyce commented. "Armando's improving! If this keeps up, he'll become almost civilized."

A few minutes later, however, when he stalked into the room, he looked anything but civilized. He seemed typecast for the dark malevolent Aztec god who took his strength from hearts sliced out of the chests of living captives.

We were still in practice clothes, but he came dressed as the living Huitzilopochtli. Black tights and leotard showed off his body. The scarlet sash circling his waist matched the red streaks that alternated with black ones on his face. He smiled at our astonishment.

"Huitzilopochtli is here!" he announced.

Joyce smiled in spite of herself.

"You didn't ride up from Sunnyvale like that! You did! Idiot! Go get warmed up!"

"Anything you say, *mi corazón*."

Although his teasing was meant for Joyce, all the time

he grinned at Kathy, signaled her with his eyes. But, chalk up one for pale little Kathy! She ignored him. Instead, she smiled hopefully at Paul, who stood in front of her at the *barre* pointedly not returning her smile.

"Hey, listen, Maggie, Joyce," Paul said after the Berkeley kids and McMichael's students had gone off to the dressing rooms, "how about coming to my place for dinner after we're through here today? To celebrate the new ballet, of course. But also for a housewarming. I've moved into a new apartment. I'd invite the whole cast, but the place is so small. Besides, I want to keep the party sort of private. But naturally, Armando, you're invited. Kathy, too, of course."

"Thanks," Armando said, bending his legs in a *plié*. We'll be there, all of us, won't we, *blanquita*?"

"Oh, yes, I'd really like that."

Kathy's long thin neck craned up at Paul, making her look pathetic, like a little girl. Her feelings for Paul were so obvious, and so unrequited! I couldn't help feeling sorry for her. I knew exactly how she felt!

While the cast was getting into costume, Joyce checked the tape deck and set the slide projector on top of a stepladder. It had to be high enough to beam the picture over the heads of the dancers.

"We aren't rehearsing down here, are we?" Armando asked, climbing up beside her to help adjust the focus of the projector. "How come we aren't using the stage where we'll be dancing tomorrow?"

"I couldn't get it. Too many others with more influence were ahead of us."

"And more *dinero* too, I'll bet. They probably have enough money for real scenery; don't have to use slides."

"This damned picture's still out of focus," Joyce said. "And stop complaining, Armando. We're lucky to have any scenery and costumes at all. We wouldn't, if it weren't for McMichael's slide projector, McMichael's tape deck, and the Indian costumes the Berkeley kids stitched up from unbleached muslin bought on sale at Woolworth's."

The costumes might be from dime-store materials, but they looked more or less authentic when I saw them on the dancers returning from the dressing room. The men wore great, broad-brimmed hats; the women tightened dark shawls over their heads and around their shoulders.

Paul, the unwilling tourist, also looked his part in belted slacks and a flowered Hawaiian shirt. Still wearing pink tights and *pointe* shoes, I stepped behind a door to slip out of my leotard and into my green dress. I carried Mama's picture hat.

"Okay. Places, everybody," Joyce called.

"Wait a minute till I pull on them white pj's over my god costume, *mujer*. And put on my hat."

He set his Mexican hat at a jaunty angle to try to attract Kathy's attention. Kathy ignored him, but he managed to annoy Joyce—which wasn't difficult this morning with all the tensions of the performance she faced, not to mention her feelings for Armando.

"Pull the hat down," Joyce said. "It has to conceal your face so that the paint can't be seen until later. You have to look like just another peasant."

Armando flipped the hat even farther back and winked at Kathy, who, bless her, lifted her little nose and settled herself against the *barre* to watch and learn the ballet.

"I'm warning you, Armando. No more clowning or I'll . . ."

Joyce didn't finish her sentence but Armando got the point. He settled the brim of the hat low over his face.

Dressed like an Indian herself, Joyce inserted a slide in

the projector and beamed onto the studio wall a Picasso-like black line drawing of a *pulquería* and a simple Mexican church. After starting the tape deck, she took her place behind the drum.

At first, no sound came, only the silence of a hot Mexican noon. Indians squatted behind imaginary wares. One woman made a tepee of her hands to suggest a pyramid of fruit. Another curled her palms to indicate the roundness of pottery bowls. I skipped among the vendors and past Indians drunk on *pulque*. Hat in hand, I let the green circle of my skirt flare around my legs.

I pointed out the wares to Paul who followed me, camera bobbing against his Hawaiian shirt. I picked up an imaginary drinking glass and with one hand sketched its tallness. But Paul was bored and hot. He wanted to get out of the sun and back to the cool hotel room.

He laid a hand on my hip, turned me toward him, rocked me, wooed me. When I snubbed him, he settled for waltzing me slowly among the Indians.

I felt their eyes on me, admiring me, I thought. The slender pretty *gringuita*. Weightless as thistledown, I soared from a *relevé* into a *fouetté*. Paul snatched me out of the air and together we spun like those little spirals of dust caught and whirled along by sudden spiteful gusts. For a second, I floated on my warm summer wind.

"Beautiful, Maggie, beautiful," Paul whispered, lapsing briefly from his role in the ballet. "Hey, wait till Randall sees you tomorrow!"

Now a single drumbeat sounded, causing the peasants to lift their heads. Slowly, as the beats became more frequent, the Indians drifted like spirits, like ghosts, toward the drum.

A line formed and a strange bent-kneed dance began. First, the males stomped alone while the females hovered on the fringe of the circle. Then, one by one, the men chose partners to create a double moving spiral, a pattern like a snail's shell.

Paul and I huddled together. We watched the slow current of the dance. Soon an Indian approached and lay his hand on one of my wrists. I drew back, alarmed but tempted.

Well, why not dance with him? When would I again be part of anything so exciting, so picturesque? I hoped Paul would snap my picture. And, later, at home, when I told this story over the bridge tables, how eyes would pop with envy! My friends would shiver and giggle with delight. "You, Maggie? Were you really that daring? Was he very attractive?" "Oh, yes," I'd say.

For this Indian, whose hat screened his face, caused stirrings in my body, stirrings never awakened by my boring little husband. Capriciously, I pushed Paul away and went with the stranger.

It took me a few minutes to learn the dance from him, but when I had, it became hypnotic. The earth itself dragged on my feet. And I was connected to this man by far more than his hand lying on my wrist.

One with each other and the earth, we stomped the long slow spiral toward the drum. Finally, as we neared the center, the notes of a flute shook me out of my dream, out of my deep trance.

The piping also released the natives. The treading circle dissolved, broke into dozens of shouting, gesturing Indians.

Beside me, my partner threw off his hat and loose white coverings and stood in skintight clothes, practically naked, a powerful male with a red-and-black streaked face. Was he man or god? When I screamed and made a feeble try to escape, he grabbed me and, with one muscular arm, thrust me high above his head.

Light blinded me, light that must come from Mc-Michael's slide projector, I knew vaguely. I was in its beam. I saw my shadow fly across the village backdrop.

Poised high in the air like a willing sacrifice, I let my skirt slide up my thighs and over my hips. Now I was spinning down across the Indian's chest. The ground came up fast, but just before I smashed into it, he halted my fall.

For a second, he held me like a butterfly speared on a pin. Close to my face grinned his wet red mouth and gleaming teeth. Then he was twisting me around his legs and between them, around his legs and between them, until I didn't know up from down, or right from left.

And didn't care. Didn't care. Let him do what he wanted. I was his. He was my demon lover.

But, suddenly, came the hoarse call of a conch shell. The Indians stopped their shouting, stopped their churning, pushed their fists high.

In the silence, the black-and-red god, my lover, again thrust me straight above his head, this time as an offering to another, greater god. Dangling there, I dimly saw what the others saw. Instead of the plaza scene, two stylized serpents zigzagged down the whitewashed wall. And between their forked and evil tongues shone a powerful head with streaming yellow hair and a light beard.

"Quetzalcoatl! Quetzalcoatl!" shouted the Indians. "The Plumed Serpent returns! The ancient gods live!"

My lover lowered me roughly onto his shoulder. Then, carrying me like a sack of meal, he again became a peasant and with the others melted out of the plaza. The Plumed Serpent vanished from the wall, where once more the church and *pulquería* appeared.

Alone in the middle of the *zócalo*, Paul shaded his eyes against the sunlight. At first he stood still, peered around him. But gradually he began running, here, there, searching, becoming more and more frantic. Where was his little wife? What had happened to her? Gone. Vanished. Disappeared. All he had left was her pretty straw hat. Finally, waving it, he rushed off to the police and joined the rest of us along the sides of the cold basement dance studio.

Chapter Eleven

After changing into street clothes, we all met across the street in the parking lot. Until everybody showed up, we waited like typical ballet dancers, toes out, waists in, chests lifted.

Then four of us climbed into Joyce's car, me in front with Joyce, Kathy scrambling in back with Paul. Armando fastened on his black helmet and mounted his motorcycle.

"Who wants to ride piggyback behind me? You, *blanquita*?"

"No way. I'm happy where I am."

"*Pelirrojita*?"

"Don't be an idiot, Armando," Joyce snapped before I could answer. Not that I would have ridden with him, of course. "Act your age. You'll simply have to ride alone."

But just as she turned on the ignition, to my astonishment, Paul opened the back door of the Chevy and, without looking at any of us, bolted toward the motorcycle.

"Hey, I'll keep you company, Armando. I've never ridden a motorcycle before. That is, if you don't mind."

Behind me, Kathy muttered something I couldn't hear.

I think Armando was as surprised as the rest of us. For a moment, he stared at Paul and then, behind his Darth Vader helmet, began to laugh.

"*Cómo no?* Why not?"

He chopped down with one foot to start the motor. Above its thunder, Paul yelled inaudibly and gestured toward the west.

The Yamaha, with us following, seemed headed for a scenic tour of the City. It ducked into the damp shadowy roads of Golden Gate Park. It raced past lakes and ponds bobbing with ducks, seagulls, and a few serene swans. It sped out of the park and along rows of houses that formed block-long walls. It turned into an emerald green golf course rimmed with black cypress trees. It climbed a hill to where the Palace of the Legion of Honor shone in the sunlight high above the blue water.

"Where the hell does he think he's going?" Kathy demanded, sulking in the back seat. "There must be a shorter way!"

Now we swung around to where we could see the ocean and bay join under the Golden Gate Bridge. Looking west, I saw a fog bank that sat on the horizon, allowing San Francisco one of its rare golden summer days.

On the lawn in front of the Palace lay dozens of couples folded together, enjoying the warmth of the day and of each other. My mind touched briefly on Doug and our long-ago picnics.

"Hurry, Joyce," I said. "They went out of sight around the next curve."

Soon we began passing blocks of stucco houses that looked as bright and clean in the sunlight as Mediterranean villas. Finally, Armando's motorcycle parked in front of a newly painted Victorian. Joyce slowed the car alongside the Yamaha.

"Around the corner and up the hill," Paul called. "You can usually find a parking space up there."

Joyce did find one, nosed the car vertically into the curb, and cramped the wheels. Armando and Paul were on the front porch waiting for us. This Victorian must have been a townhouse, but now, judging from the number of mailboxes and doorbells, it was divided into three apartments.

Paul unlocked the door and led us up a polished wooden staircase that narrowed after it passed the second story. On the third level, he opened a carved oak door and stood back to let us pass inside.

We entered a large living room. Paul's invitation was not as spur of the moment as it had seemed, for he was obviously prepared for us. In the center of the room stood a table covered with a dark green cloth and set for six. We were only five, so he must be expecting a sixth guest.

A pair of silver candles rose from pewter holders. They repeated the grays and blacks of the wallpaper's rather harsh geometric design. The tableware was heavy glossy stainless steel. The dishes and, of course, the wineglasses were all clear glass. Between the candlesticks, in a half-liter wine decanter, curled a smooth, waxy blossom that looked like a calla lily, only it was black.

"How elegant, Paul," Joyce said, pausing in the doorway. "Everything. Did you have a decorator?"

"Oh, you must have," I said. "No offense, Paul, but your old place was nothing like this!"

"I'll say not," Kathy said. "It was just like any other dancer's pad. Old sofa, beat-up table, mismatched chairs. And the clothes line. Always the clothes line. Dripping with all sorts of tights and leg warmers. Did your mother increase your allowance, Paul? This place even has a view. How about showing it to me?"

"I'll be glad to, *blanquita*, while Paul is busy with his other guests."

Armando tried to press her toward the window, but she stepped aside and Joyce said sharply, "It's Paul's apartment so it's his privilege to show off his view."

"Yes, so show it to me, Paul," Kathy said.

"Hey, I'll show it to everybody. Though it's not the greatest!"

We all followed him to one of the two bay windows—all except Kathy who sulked beside the table, fingering the black lily.

Paul's view consisted mostly of an unbroken row of Victorian houses opposite his own, but far to the right, the street seemed to dive off into the bay. Beyond that, stretched a band of blue-gray hills.

When we turned back into the room, Kathy had disappeared, but I heard her in the bathroom. When she finished, I went in to try to tame my hair which the damp wind had whipped into strawberry froth. The tiny room was pale green. Its fixtures, like pieces in a three-dimensional puzzle, were arranged in the only way they could possibly fit.

After washing my hands and face, I dried them on a soft green towel laid out on the tub with the foresight my mother might have shown. But Paul? After unsuccessfully trying to pull a comb through my hair, I finally just tied a scarf over it.

On my way back to the living room, I peeked into the kitchen. It was painted pale yellow and looked immaculate, uncooked in. Not a dish on the green-tiled counter, not a pan on the shining stainless-steel stove or in the glistening microwave oven. Maybe Paul was having the dinner catered. I hadn't realized that the allowance his mother sent him was so large. Another door, which must lead into his bedroom, was closed.

The candles were burning palely on the green table when I returned to the main room. Everybody stood around sipping white wine while Paul set out individual bowls of salad and two large straw baskets. One contained slices of warm sourdough French bread, the other a jumble of the disassembled legs and bodies of several dungeness crabs. Paul must have prepared the whole meal this morning and hidden it away in the refrigerator. An instant in the microwave would have warmed the bread.

"Everything's beautiful, perfect, Paul. I especially like the view," Joyce said.

"Yeah, someday you'll make someone a good wife. Or roommate," Kathy said, blinking her pale lashes at him. "How about me?"

She pretended it was a joke but everybody knew she was serious, including Paul. A blush crept up his throat.

"Thanks, but I'm already spoken for."

"You've got to be kidding!"

"Come on, Kathy, stop bugging Paul," Joyce said. "We're here to help him warm his new apartment."

"Hey, that's okay, Joyce. As a matter of fact, I really do have a new roommate. He prepared all this."

Paul's gesture included room, decorations, food.

"Oh, just a roommate," Kathy said. "That's a relief. I got the idea you were getting married or something. This roommate of yours must be pretty terrific to change your life this much. I'd like to meet him."

"He should be back any minute," Paul said. "He left a note saying he had gone to get some champagne."

Then, at the sound of a key turning in the lock, Paul flushed again.

"Here comes my roommate now."

He went to the door to let in a slightly built man with short ginger-colored hair and freckles.

"Seth!" Kathy cried.

I knew him too, of course; he was one of the students from the ballet school and, like Paul, a new apprentice. We also knew that he was gay.

"Yes. Seth and I are roommates. And we hope, we both hope that you'll all drink to our happiness together."

I was surprised about Paul. But now I understood the closed look that sometimes came into his eyes, filming over their clear blueness.

"It sounds like you're announcing your engagement or something," Kathy said, her hands going to her ears, sliding down her scarlet cheeks. "Anyway, I'm not feeling so good, got a headache, so if everybody will excuse me . . ."

She ran crookedly to the door and tried to wrench it open.

"Oh, shit! Can somebody help me get out of here?"

Armando was there, opening the door.

"I'll just see that she gets home okay."

I saw Joyce bite her lip to keep from commenting. Then she lifted her chin. She held out her glass for Paul to fill.

"How about some of that champagne?" she said. "I want to make a toast. To Paul and Seth, their apartment, and their life together. And while we're at it, to Maggie and me, too. Things are bound to get better soon."

Chapter Twelve

On the Sunday morning of the Competition, I awoke depressed and exhausted. Maybe I had celebrated too much at Paul's party or had to get up too early to drive to the City. Maybe I was simply tired from too much rehearsing, too much worry. Worry, for one thing, about whether Armando after disappearing with Kathy would show up at the Competition. For Joyce, of course, the worry must have been tenfold.

And we had good reason to worry. Half an hour before our ballet was scheduled to go on, Armando and Kathy had still not arrived. The rest of us limbered up down in the icy cellar where the cold of the concrete floor seemed to enter my muscles.

"Damn them," Joyce said. "Well, get into your costumes, kids. We'll go upstairs. They may still show up."

We carried our equipment up to the cold drafty hall and tried to keep our muscles warm outside the double classroom which today was transformed into a stage and auditorium. From the door leading to the performing area came whiny electronic music to which the first group of our competitors must be moving.

Soon applause pattered and a handful of sweating dancers came out the stage door. They were in red tights and red leotards, which were painted, for deep symbolic reasons, no doubt, with huge black cabbages.

They were replaced by seven dancers in long white tutus. After a period of silence, during which, I suppose, the choreographer of their ballet was interviewed by the judges, I heard a faint tinkling of Chopin.

"My God, our turn's next," Joyce said. "I'll kill Armando."

But at that moment, we heard the rumbling of a motor-cycle, then a door slam followed by footsteps on the stairs. Finally, his face painted but still in street clothes, Armando sauntered, hand-in-hand with Kathy, into the hall.

When Joyce spotted them, she turned away. Couldn't Armando, for heaven's sake, have resisted flaunting his new girl friend? Especially today? Kathy, at least, did have the grace to blush.

Then Armando dropped her hand and, as if nothing had changed, put an arm around Joyce.

"Sorry, *mujer*. We got held up in traffic."

Joyce shook away his arm and went to check the tape deck.

"Look, Joyce, I said I was sorry. What more do you want?"

In silence, she tested the switch of the projector.

"Shit. If that's the way you're going to be, *mujer!*"

"Look, Armando," I said, "why don't you just get into your costume and shut up? We go on in less than ten minutes."

"Okay. Okay. So I was a little late."

He stalked off. To the dressing room, I hoped. But, there stood Kathy, leaning against the wall in jeans and T-shirt. From under her corn-colored lashes she peered at Paul, but turned her head when he happened to look in her direction.

"Don't you think you'd better put on practice clothes and warm up?" I snapped.

But I should be collecting myself, concentrating on the role I was to dance, doing a few more *pliés* and *tendus* and *petit battements*. Something, anything, to melt the icy stiffness out of my limbs and body. Not to mention my mind.

Now faint applause replaced the tinkling Chopin. The stage door opened and a second group of sweating dancers emerged.

"Okay, kids," Joyce told us. "Places. I'll handle the tape deck, of course, and check the lighting. But, George," she said to one of the dancers from Berkeley, "you set the drum. You know where it goes, precisely at center stage. I chalked an X there yesterday, but it's probably been smudged away. And, Paul, will you take care of the stepladder and focus the projector? Thanks."

"But, *mujer*, I'm in charge of the drum and projector," said Armando, back from the dressing room in costume.

She sent him a quick hot look, then repeated her requests to George and Paul.

We moved to the stage on which we had not been allowed to rehearse. But I knew every stain and board of its dark wooden floor because this stage was the classroom where I had taken daily classes for the last three years with Madame Martina.

It rose three steps above a second classroom. This morning the two studios were separated by heavy cotton curtains instead of the usual accordian-pleated divider.

"Open the curtains," called a voice from the lower classroom. The voice was Randall's.

I wasn't surprised, only terrified. Joyce looked as if someone had stabbed her.

"But we're not ready yet," she cried, apparently having forgotten, during those last frantic moments, about the preliminary interview that was required.

"No matter. No matter. Please open the curtains. We talk to all the participants before they perform. And we're especially eager to chat with you. This is the only ballet by a woman to make the finals."

Joyce said to us, "Places, everybody. This shouldn't take long. Okay, now the curtain."

A thin boy, a student in the ballet class below mine, opened it.

"Good morning," said Larry Randall.

From my corner, I quickly spotted his blond head at a long table set in the center of the lower classroom.

To his right sat the company director, Robert Morris, and next to Morris, rose the ancient skull of Leonide Lermontov, a teacher who nearly a century ago danced with the Marinsky Ballet in St. Petersburg. On Randall's left was Terrence Chagall, the school director, and next to him, Eleanora Martina, his wife who had been my teacher.

"Randall and his silent partners," Paul whispered. He stood beside me in the corner ready for our first cue. "The others must detest public speaking!"

"Well, at least I have one friend there," I said. "Madame Martina likes me."

"Chagall and Morris, too. And old Lermontov always gave you lots of attention in his partnering classes."

Students from the summer school and parents and friends of the competing choreographers filled the rest of the studio. I spotted Seth's ginger-colored head a few yards behind the judges' table.

"Would the person who did the choreography for this ballet please step forward?" Randall called. "Good morning. You're dressed in white trousers like a man, but you're listed here as Joyce Mallory. Is that correct? Good. You'll notice, Miss Mallory—or is it Mrs.?"

I could tell that he didn't recognize her, but she knew and loathed him because of his arrogance years before when he had guest-starred with our little company down the Peninsula. Her dislike showed in the dryness of her replies.

"Ms., if you please, Mr. Randall."

"If you insist. Ms. As I was saying, Ms. Mallory, I asked for 'the person who did the choreography.' You'll notice that I didn't call you a choreographer because, as with the title ballerina, choreographer is reserved for the proven few: for Balanchine, Petipa, Fokine, Massine, Tudor, Ashton. To name only a handful. Some might add de Mille and Nijinska, but I don't include those two ladies. I consider their ballets too uneven, too flawed. But let's see what you have to offer, Miss—I beg your pardon —Ms. Mallory."

"You're very kind, Mr. Randall."

She enunciated her words clearly, drily, but I could hear the shake of anger in her voice. It echoed mine. The chauvinist! The woman-hater!

"I see you have called your entry *The Plumed Serpent*, Ms. Mallory, or *Quetzal* . . . however you pronounce it. And yet this name doesn't appear among the list of characters you submitted. Would you care to explain?"

From my corner, I saw her lift her chin.

"I believe, Mr. Randall, that if you'll allow us to proceed, the ballet will be self-explanatory."

Good for her. Oh, good for Joyce! Randall gave a choke of laughter.

"I admire your self-confidence, your poise, Ms. Mallory, especially since I notice that you're not a company member or a student from our school."

"No, Mr. Randall, I'm a student at Cal—the University of California at Berkeley."

"Admirable. Admirable. We're honored to have an intellectual among our contestants. And looking over the names you have listed in your cast, I assume that most of your dancers also are from the University. I recognize only two from this school. Paul Lawrence, one of our new apprentices, and Maggie Adams."

At his mention of my name, I shrank farther into the corner.

"Hey, relax, Maggie. You'll be great. Just like yesterday," Paul whispered.

"I didn't realize the Competition was so parochial, Mr. Randall, that the applicants were limited to your company and school," Joyce said.

Robert Morris stood up then.

"They're not limited at all, Ms. Mallory. You're very welcome. So if we may have the curtains closed, we'll watch your ballet with a great deal of interest. We were very impressed with the tape you submitted."

After the boy closed the curtain, Paul rushed up the ladder to project the drawing of the plaza church and *pulquería* on the white backdrop. Joyce squinted at the overhead lights and asked the boy to dim them.

"Dimmer yet, please."

"That's as dim as they go, ma'am."

"Shit. I guess they'll have to do."

She started the tape, crouched behind the drum, and signaled for the curtain. I crossed my fingers, breathed deeply, and skipped forward while laughing back at Paul. Then, suddenly, I tripped over the foot of one of the vendors. I recovered quickly, but, looking under the Indian's hat, I met Armando's eyes. He grinned. Oh, damn him! Had he done it on purpose?

I showed Paul the imaginary pottery, the pyramided fruit, but the part wasn't working for me. I wasn't into it.

Paul and I began to waltz, but I kept worrying about Randall out there in the audience.

"Hey, relax, Maggie, you're doing fine," Paul whispered. But I knew I wasn't. He tightened his hold on the the small of my back. "Now, get ready for the lift."

I pulled in my waist, raised my chest, but, dear God, when I whirled into the *fouetté*, I felt a searing pull. Then I was in Paul's arms.

"My ankle. It's my stupid ankle!"

"Okay, Maggie, okay. Relax. Trust me."

But, instead of continuing to waltz among the vendors, Paul circled to the stage door, carrying me in his arms. Over my protests, he opened it and set me down in the hallway.

"Where's Kathy?" he demanded, breathing hard, an arm still supporting me. He searched among the waiting dancers. "Kathy, where the hell are you?"

"I can do it, Paul," I said. "It isn't that bad. The waltz is almost over, anyway. Let me go back."

"No. Your *pas de deux* with Armando is too demanding, it might cause permanent injury. Where is that stupid Kathy?"

I saw her come out of the lower classroom and hurry toward us.

"What's wrong?"

"Get over here," Paul said, zipping open my long back fastener. He stripped off my dress. "Listen, Kathy, don't you know understudies are supposed to stick around?"

"I was only watching the ballet. I came as soon as I saw you and Maggie duck out. What's the matter?"

"Never mind. Get into Maggie's costume."

"But I'm not warmed up!"

"Too bad."

He pulled my dress over Kathy's head and tried to zip it up.

"Tuck in your waist, for crying out loud. The costume's too tight, but you'll have to wear it. Give her the hat, Maggie. And someone take care of this girl," he said to the waiting dancers. "She's hurt."

He picked up Kathy and rushed with her back through the stage door just as the first drum beat sounded.

Crying, naked to the waist, I leaned against the wall, my weight on my uninjured right foot. A girl from the company wrapped her shawl around me.

The flute soon joined the drum, signaling my *pas de deux* with Armando, now Kathy's *pas de deux* with Armando. Then came the call of the conch shell. Then applause. Louder than for the other ballets. Or did my biased imagination only make it seem louder? Now the dancers from *Serpent* crowded out into the hall. There came Kathy in my dress and Armando, grinning under his red-and-black face paint. Finally, I saw Paul with the ladder and projector, and Joyce carrying the tape deck.

"How did it go?" I asked.

Joyce made a leveling gesture with one hand. "So-so."

"It was great!" Paul said.

"That's what I was—great! Armando, the Great! But how's the ankle, *pelirrojita*? Let me get you downstairs."

"Hey, I'll do that!"

Despite Paul's protests, Armando carried me gently downstairs and seated me in a chair near Joyce.

"Well, thanks, Armando," she said, stepping out of her costume. "That must be your good deed for the day. Or did you have ulterior motives? Mag, I feel terrible about your foot. It must have been rehearsing on that concrete floor. I'm getting you to a doctor right away."

"But what about the Competition? The results?" I asked.

"They won't know until they've seen all the ballets, anyway."

"Hey, you stay here, Joyce," Paul said. "Let Seth and me take Maggie to the doctor. If you'll let us borrow your car, that is."

Nearby, Armando took off his white pajamas.

"I'll drive her, *mujer*."

"Not in my mother's car!" Joyce said, tossing her keys to Paul. "And not on your motorcycle either. We want Mag back safely. Besides, how can you spare the time away from your current girl friend?"

"Okay. Okay. I get the picture."

Kathy came out of the dressing room in street clothes. She hooked an arm through one of Armando's.

"Come on, honey. Let's go," she said.

Armando looked at Joyce, his dark face expressionless.

"Is it okay if we split now?"

"Why ask me, lover boy?"

Then she said to Paul, "I'll have Mag ready in a minute."

She helped me to the dressing room.

"I'm really sorry, Joyce. About letting you down. About Armando too."

"You couldn't help the ankle, Mag. As for Armando, well, I've really known from the beginning how it would end. But, why Kathy? Though I really should feel sorry for her. And look at the mess she made of your dress."

I saw it lying in a green pool on the dressing room floor.

Chapter Thirteen

A few hours later, when Paul and Seth brought me back from the company doctor, my left foot, ankle, and leg up to the knee were in a light cast.

"My God, is it that bad?" Joyce asked when I swung into the crowded foyer on a pair of crutches. "Did you break something, Mag?"

"No, but I sprained my stupid ankle and strained the tendon pretty badly, the doctor says."

"And since she didn't follow her dad's orders and get lots of rest this summer," Paul said, helping me onto one of the sofas, "the doc fixed her up real good! In a cast for three weeks, and absolutely no dancing for six."

"Oh, Mag, I shouldn't have insisted you do *Serpent*!"

"I'd have taken class or something anyway."

"Your dad'll have a fit."

"So, what else is new?"

"Mag, I'm sorry. What'll you do for six weeks?"

I shrugged. What would I do? No Doug. No apprenticeship. Now, absolutely no dancing. I remembered how bored I was the last time I had sprained my ankle, the same ankle, exactly three years ago, a few hours before I was supposed to dance in another of Joyce's ballets. Then I was only a kid, only fifteen. But eighteen was really as late as most professional companies wanted to accept apprentices and *corps* members. And here I was on crutches again!

"What'll I do? Go crazy, I suppose."

"No, you won't, Maggie," Paul said. "You'll rest and read and be ready to start dancing again in September."

He placed a duffel bag under my damaged foot. Seth leaned my crutches against the wall, out of the way of the dancers crowding the foyer.

"Any news yet?" I asked Joyce.

"No. They just saw the last entry and must be conferring now."

I looked around at the waiting dancers. Some chattered, a few paced, others sat on chairs, sofas, or crosslegged on the floor, drinking diet sodas or black coffee from styrofoam cups. I recognized students from this school and a few company members, but nobody from *Serpent* except Paul, who had just returned with me.

"Were you here all alone?" I asked. "Nobody waited with you?"

"Well, the minibus took the kids back down the Peninsula, but most of the Berkeley people are around somewhere. And, if you mean Armando—no, he and Kathy haven't returned. And good riddance!"

I reached down to shift my left leg to a more comfortable position. My ankle was beginning to hurt.

"Hey, I think the waiting is about over," Paul said. "Here comes Randall parading down the stairs. Da-da-da-duh!"

I watched the assistant director's loose-hipped walk, his arrogant blond head, and his chiseled profile. He was considered handsome by a following of female ballet fans. Little did they know!

At the front desk, Randall switched on the loud speaker.

"Good afternoon, ladies and gentlemen. After much deliberation, the judges have reached a decision. May I

106

ask those with entries in the Competition to assemble immediately upstairs in the lower classroom? Interested spectators are also invited."

Joyce took a step toward the staircase, then returned to the three of us with a deprecating little laugh.

"I'm scared to death. Could somebody please come along to hold my hand, figuratively, of course?"

"Hey, I'll come. If it's okay with you, Maggie. Seth can stay down here with you," Paul said.

"But I want to come too!" I said.

I had two reasons. The obvious one, of course, was to find out if Joyce's ballet had won. The second reason was more tenuous. During the long hours of rehearsal, a tiny hope kept burning. Maybe, just maybe, after seeing my performance, those judges would relent, would award me an apprenticeship. This morning, of course, I got hurt and couldn't perform. But three years ago, although the same thing happened, I had received a scholarship to this school anyway.

"Hand me my crutches, will you, Seth?"

"No way, Maggie," Paul said. "I'll carry you upstairs. Seth can bring along your crutches."

When most of the people had funneled up the staircase, Paul lifted me in his arms and the four of us followed the crowd upstairs and into the classroom.

We found chairs near the door. The judges were now up on the stage, seated behind their long table. Just as Randall pounded his gavel, Armando and Kathy edged into the room. With them, to my surprise, was Lupe, looking thin and big-eyed. Joyce and I exchanged glances, but Randall was starting to speak.

"Determining the best of these final entries has not been an easy task, let me assure you, ladies and gentle-men. The styles varied from jazz to classical to ethnic.

107

But after a struggle, we have settled on one winner and two runners-up."

Beside me, Joyce groaned and bit her thumbnail.

"An interesting aspect of all three winning ballets—an aspect which certainly contributes to their freshness and originality—is the combining of at least two dance forms in a single work."

I gave Joyce a quick hug.

"You're a winner!"

"Don't jump to conclusions, Mag!"

But I heard the hope in her voice.

"The way we'll do this, ladies and gentlemen," Randall continued, "is to name the two runners-up first, ask them to—well—run up (ha-ha) to receive their checks and plaques. And then we'll announce the person whose work City Ballet will produce."

"I can't stand it!" Joyce said. "If I smoked, I'd go out for a cigarette!"

Instead, she chewed what was left of her thumbnail, while Randall called up a balding young company soloist, whose skin was the same blue-white shade as the skim milk I drink to keep my weight down. His ballet, apparently the Chopin work danced just before *Serpent*, won third place. Second prize went to a Japanese, also a company member, for a ballet called *Faded Dreams*.

"It's all or nothing, then!" Joyce said.

She reached for my hand, crushed it within hers, while we awaited the announcement of the top winner. Obviously delighting in the drama, the tension, the torture he was inflicting, Randall banged the gavel for silence.

"Finally, ladies and gentlemen, we come to the supreme moment, the moment we've all been waiting for. Would Nathan Summers please step forward. Mr. Summers' astonishing work . . ."

But I refused to hear about Nathan Summers' astonishing work. For one thing, Nathan Summers, another
rapidly rising young soloist in the company, was a favorite of Randall. I put an arm around Joyce.

"It's favoritism, not to mention male chauvinism!
Serpent is good—the best!"

"Don't, Mag!"

"Let's get out of here."

"Not yet. I can't. I won't walk out."

Beside me, her strong profile faced the judges' table. I
saw the winner bound to the stage, saw his ecstatic grin,
saw him pumping hands with all the judges. Finally,
Randall draped an arm around his shoulders and raised a
hand for silence.

"Ladies and gentlemen! Ladies and gentlemen! One
minute please. Our panel of judges reminds me that we
have one more award to make: Honorable Mention for
the most unusual ballet goes to Joyce Mallory for *The
Plumed Serpent*, a very interesting, if not fully realized,
work. We hope Miss—Ms. Mallory will submit other ballets in future competitions. The judges believe her choreography shows considerable promise."

For a minute Joyce only sat there.

"I don't know whether I've been patted on the back or
slapped in the face. Both, I guess. But it's better than
nothing!"

"Yes, but you should have placed first!" I said.

Following a patter of applause, Randall pounded the
gavel again.

"Let me make a few further comments about Ms. Mallory's ballet. Its most original aspect was its use of classical ballet contrasted with an ancient Indian circle dance.
The work suffered, however, from a lack of clarity as to
intent. Another weakness, not inherent in the ballet, of

course, was the inexplicable rush offstage of one of the leads who was replaced by a dancer who seemed totally unfamiliar with the role. We suspect an injury, but the understudy should have been able to carry through the part more convincingly. However, again on the plus side, Ms. Mallory's ballet did allow us to spot a dancer who shows extraordinary talent."

Dear God, in spite of everything, was my hope about to be realized?

"We are awarding a full ballet scholarship plus living stipend to Armando Flores for his strong performance as the Aztec god in Ms. Mallory's *The Plumed Serpent*. Please stand up, Mr. Flores."

"The little shit!" Joyce said. "But he is fantastically talented."

I could have said, "So am I! Oh, so am I!" But I didn't.

Two rows ahead of us Armando freed himself from Kathy's hug, stood up, bowed modestly, and sat down again between Kathy and Lupe. He didn't look back at us, but maybe he hadn't seen us. Anyway, I hated him!

When people began crowding around the winners, Joyce said, "I'll have to congratulate him."

"Him? He should congratulate you! And thank you. At least, thank you."

"Fierce loyal Mag! And he will! He'll thank me most charmingly. Watch and see."

Followed by Paul, Joyce started toward Armando.

"You stay here with Maggie," Paul called back to Seth.

"No, I'm coming too," answered Seth who was usually so docile.

Paul raised his eyebrows. "Well, whatever you say, Seth. Here comes Lupe to keep Maggie company, anyway."

Lupe looked at the cast on my foot.

"Poor Maggie! When Armando and Kathy told me about your ankle I came right back with them. I'm so sorry. Does it hurt much?"

"It hurts, but what really hurts is not being able to dance."

"I know, *cariña*. That's why I came back last night. I decided I couldn't give up dancing, not even for Eddy."

"You broke up with him then?"

"Yes. And our wedding date was all set and everything. The second Friday in September, it was going to be."

The tears shining in her eyes made them seem enormous, like the huge eyes of waifs photographed for Save the Children appeals.

"But I couldn't go through with it, Maggie. I just couldn't. He believes dancing is bad, evil. Sinful, he says, 'cause it shows off your body, gives you lustful thoughts. But Eddy says it's not too late for me. I could still be saved if I repent and come to the Lord. And, of course, not dance no more!"

Tears ran down her face. She shook her head.

"But, Maggie, you and the little kids in class and the dancers in the company, you're not sinful and lustful. And ballet don't make me feel wicked and lustful either. When I dance, I feel pure and light and, well, spiritual, lifted up to heaven."

"Sure, Lupe. You feel lifted towards heaven the same as I feel lifted on my summer wind. I guess, for us, dancing's a religion."

"Eddy, he also said to throw away my St. Christopher medal. He says, wearing it is the same as worshipping idols. Finally, I couldn't take it no more. And I told him so. And do you know what he said? 'I'm sorry you feel that way, Lupe. I'm only trying to bring you to the Lord, to save your immortal soul.' "

"Poor Lupe."

"Yes, well, it's hard 'cause I love Eddy a lot. I really do. But I'll be okay. I know I will. As soon as I start dancing again, practicing, rehearsing. But, poor Maggie, with your ankle, you can't even dance!"

Chapter Fourteen

"Poor Maggie!" Lupe had said that terrible Sunday in August. "I don't have Eddy no more, but you can't dance."

And I'm afraid I spent a week saying the same thing to myself, hobbling around the house, watching soap operas, rocking myself in the big creaky old swing on the patio, and gaining weight.

"Get hold of yourself, Maggie," my father said, looking across his newspaper one morning at breakfast. "Go take a typing class at the junior college."

"Father! You're so predictable. I could have bet you'd say that."

"Good. I'm glad you can depend on me. So why don't you take a typing class at the junior college?"

"It's too late. The summer session's nearly over. Besides I don't want to."

He sent a questioning look at Mama who was trying to hide a smile.

"Maggie's right, dear. Classes really are over. It's almost the middle of August."

"Well, try the playground then. Maybe there are classes there. It's not good for you to mope around feeling sorry for yourself. Get out of the house. It's your left foot, so you could drive your mother's car with the automatic transmission."

After he left, Mama arched an eyebrow at me.

"How about it, Maggie? Want to use my car?"

"Where would I go? Though I really would like to see Father's face if I got a job at McDonald's. But with one foot in a cast I can't even do that."

"Maybe you could help out at McMichael's? Answer his phone? Take roll?"

"That would make me feel even worse, being around dancing, but not able to dance."

"Well, Maggie, I understand that he needs someone. The mothers who usually help out are away on vacation until after Labor Day."

"Mama, you've talked to him already!"

"Well, look at it this way, honey, he needs help and so do you."

That's how I happened to be taking a coffee break in the doughnut shop across the street from the ballet school one hot afternoon late in August. I sat across from Joyce, who was living at home, studying at McMichael's, and trying to get over Armando before fall quarter started at Cal. We had been sitting there only a few minutes when in walked Doug.

I hadn't seen him for nearly two months, since my birthday in fact, but the sight of his red beard, his lankiness, and the quick duck of his head to avoid the door frame made my heart leap to my throat. He wasn't alone, but at least he wasn't with Charmaine or some other girl.

With him was a man, much older, as old as my father. Doug was wearing an open-collared sport shirt and white jeans but his friend looked hot and uncomfortable in a light suit. Was he a relative or friend Doug had just picked up at the airport?

Doug didn't see me at first. Then he did. He halted. His face blazed as if a flashbulb had gone off a few feet from him. Then, of course, he calmed down, smiled at me, nodded politely to Joyce, sat down with his friend two tables away. But, happy, happy day! I had seen his first delight, his initial excitement!

"That's your Doug, isn't it, Mag?"

"Not *my* Doug."

"I saw his face. He'll come around fast."

I ate my doughnut slowly, used my finger to mop up the raspberry jelly that had spilled onto the fluted paper plate, and tried to think of a way to bring Doug over. Finally, it was my cast that did it. All at once he was beside me, bending over to look at the horrid thing.

"Mag, what happened?"

When I told him, he looked sympathetic.

"Then you can't dance."

"Not for a while, but I get the cast off next Friday."

He looked at Joyce and then at the man he had left two tables away.

"Maybe we can get together sometime. It'll have to be soon though. In three weeks I leave for MIT."

Three weeks! Of course, I knew about MIT. I remembered way back in June, hearing him tell Mama he was going there. At the time, though, the whole endless summer spread before us like a garden filled with flowers waiting to be picked. And we had wasted all of it. Or nearly all. Now instead of three long months, only three weeks remained. Three short weeks!

"That man's from MIT. He's making a short stopover here to talk about the program I've been accepted in. He'll be my advisor."

"Oh."

"But I'll phone you tonight as soon as I put him on the plane, Mag. Okay?"

That evening I did nothing except wait for Doug to

115

phone. Late August had turned hot and we were without air conditioning because my father didn't believe in it, said it harmed the sinuses. Mama had turned out all the lights and opened all the doors and windows to let in any coolness, any breeze that might be stirring down from the dry foothills or off our shallow end of the bay.

But instead of coolness, hot darkness entered with all the night noises. Crickets. Oak leaves clicking. One shrill, lonely bird call. Neighbors' voices out on their patios. Screams and laughter from a swimming party down the block. An occasional car motor. And the far-off hum of traffic along El Camino Real.

"It's cooler out on the patio now," Mama said, passing through the dark entry hall where I lay in shorts and halter on the tile floor near the phone. She was going to the kitchen to get my father another beer.

"It's not bad in the den either where we're watching tennis on TV."

"I'm fine, Mama. I think there's a tiny breeze coming through the front door."

"All right, dear. But is something wrong?"

"No. Except that Doug said he would phone."

I hope I sounded okay, not all tied up like I felt.

"Doug?"

"I saw him today."

"Oh, well, I hope he doesn't wait too long. Your father's going to bed soon."

At ten o'clock, my father came through the hall to take his beer cans back to the kitchen.

"What are you doing down there on the floor?"

"Keeping cool, Father."

"Well, it's time to go to bed."

"It's too hot."

"That may be, but your mother and I are going to bed.

116

I'm getting up at five. I want to play tennis before it gets too hot. So I'll let you lock up. Don't forget."

Still the phone didn't ring, but after the bathroom noises, the talking, the rustlings of my parents going to bed finally ended, I saw headlights beam into the driveway. A car bounded up and stopped. In the hot night, the car door closing sounded like an explosion. Then I felt, rather than saw, a tall shadow crossing the lawn to the open front door.

I was up, leaning on one crutch, hardly breathing, waiting inside the hooked screen door when the black silhouette came onto the porch and hesitated. I could hear rapid breathing.

"Doug?"

"Mag. Your house is all dark. I was afraid you weren't home. Or had gone to bed."

"My parents are in bed. I nearly went too."

"I'm sorry. My advisor's plane was late and I had to wait with him. Then I decided to rush over without calling. Are you going to let me in?"

I unhooked the screen, but instead of letting him in, I hobbled out, taking along only one crutch.

Doug didn't hug or kiss me, but he did take my hand, the one that wasn't holding onto the cross-dowel of the crutch. We started walking away from the house.

"Mag, all evening I've been thinking about us and what went wrong in June. I decided that we should start all over again. Pretend we just met this afternoon, not in the doughnut shop, but in some resort, in Honolulu, in Puerto Vallarte, and have only a three-week vacation to spend together. We have no past, no future, only the here and now."

"What for? It sounds crazy."

"Well, I think that was our trouble back in June. We

117

were bringing up things from when we were just kids. Problems over your ballet. And expecting each other to have been on ice all those years. Maybe that was why we couldn't handle Charmaine or the blond boy."

"Paul. But Paul's gay."

"That's not important now. Let's clean the slate. No Paul. No Charmaine. No ballet."

I stopped under the tent of the giant oak.

"Maybe no ballet right now, Doug, but after my ankle heals . . ."

"Okay, but for tonight, for these three weeks, it's just you and me, Mag, getting acquainted and being together."

"But it's not the way things really are. It's not true."

"Sure, it's true. We're who we are now and we have three weeks."

It sounded crazy, like some philosophical idea Joyce might have picked up over at Cal, but I let him keep my hand. At the base of the tree, we sat down on one of its huge, twisted roots. Above our heads, the oak's leaves chattered and a faint wind sang high in its crown.

I rolled out onto the lawn and lay flat on my stomach. Following me, Doug pressed his face between my shoulder blades. I felt his beard on my bare back and his lips brushing my skin.

"Mag, we'll make the most of our three weeks, okay?"

He turned me over and began kissing my mouth. And his kissing was even more exciting than I remembered. Gentle. Soft. Coaxing. But he stopped almost immediately.

"Oh boy!" he said. "Looks like we're in for it. Your parents are up."

Lights yellowed window after window. Through the open front door, they cast a long rectangle of shine across

118

the walk and over the grass. Wearing only pajama bottoms, my father stood in the bright doorway, peering into the darkness.

"Maggie, you forgot to lock up. Where are you, Maggie?"

Doug rolled away from me, but I took hold of his arm.

"Don't go, Doug. He can't see us."

"No. I'd better leave. Here, let me help you up."

He gently freed himself from my hold and set me on my feet. He settled the crutch under my right arm.

"Good night, Mag."

"Will I see you tomorrow?"

"What do you think? Now, I'll try to make a quiet getaway. Steal silently into the night."

Chapter Fifteen

Doug coasted his car out of our driveway and down the slight incline of the street. He didn't start his motor until he was three houses away, but he didn't fool my father.

"Who were you with out there?"

He opened the screen door for me.

"Nobody."

"Don't lie. I saw somebody cross the lawn and a car roll away."

"Well, Doug."

"Doug? If it was Doug, why didn't you ask him in?"

"Father, it was Doug. Who do you think?"

My father shrugged his heavy, freckled shoulders. He hitched up his wine-red pajama bottoms.

"I can't understand why you didn't ask him in, that's all, if it was Doug."

I limped off toward my room.

"I give up. I tell you the truth but you don't believe me."

When I got up the next morning my father had gone, but Mama was there. She wasn't taking classes this summer and sat across the breakfast table from me, drinking her coffee.

"Your father says you told him Doug was here last night."

"Yes. Doug didn't phone after all. He just came. I

don't know why Father won't believe that it was Doug out in front with me."

Mama laughed gently.

"Fathers always suspect the worst. He thinks it was the Mexican boy, the one who came here to your birthday party."

"Armando?"

"Yes. He doesn't trust Armando."

"Neither do I. He is honest though! But he's in San Francisco and I was out there with Doug. We didn't want to wake you and Father."

"Thank you for being so extremely considerate."

"It's true. Or half true. I really like him, Mama."

While my mind went back to last night and his soft, delicious kisses, I saw Mama frowning and stirring her coffee.

"Before I started to college at the ripe old age of forty and got to know a lot of young people, I wouldn't have dreamed of saying what I'm going to say now, Maggie. I would simply have warned you against too much kissing, too much necking, as we used to call it. But going to college has taught me at least this: to warn a daughter is useless, completely ineffective. So, since I'm now an enlightened mother, I'm suggesting that you go down to Planned Parenthood in case you and Doug get carried away."

I looked up startled, shocked really, and I think I blushed.

"Mama, you're jumping to conclusions."

"Just as a precaution, honey."

"Mama, Doug and I have never gone beyond kissing."

Which was not entirely true. In high school we used to do a little touching, but last night we had only started to kiss when my father got up and practically turned our place into the Pigeon Point Lighthouse, for God's sake.

122

"Maggie, you're both older now. It's true you've been wrapped up in ballet, been practically a nun, as far as I know. But Doug's been away at the University for two years."

"Are you accusing Doug of sleeping with all sorts of girls?"

I was indignant, but really I was only attributing to her my own suspicions, especially about Doug and Charmaine.

"I'm not accusing anyone of anything, Maggie. I'm only saying, as a precaution, pay a visit to Planned Parenthood. Which doesn't mean you must sleep with him, or that I give you my permission to sleep with him. In fact, if you were to ask me, which is very unlikely, I would say: Don't—at least not until you're ready to make a commitment. But I want you to be safe, so you'd better go down to Planned Parenthood."

I did. I stopped on my way to McMichael's and when Doug came over that night I was shy and nervous, but prepared. All we did, though, was hold hands through some dull movie at the Century 22 and have doughnuts and coffee at the doughnut shop.

Later, parked in front of my house, he did kiss me slowly, while his hands stroked and touched me, but just as I was melting against him, he gave me a quick brotherly hug.

"I'd better be going, Mag."

"What? How come you're in such a rush?"

"Well, I wouldn't mind kissing you like that all night, but I don't want your dad to get any wrong ideas."

He helped me out of the car and handed me my crutches.

"Good night, Mag. See you tomorrow."

He gunned away while I stared after him. I was annoyed and confused. If we really were playing his here-and-now game with no yesterdays and especially no tomorrows, why did he care what my father thought? A few minutes later, though, I couldn't help feeling better because, at the corner, he tooted me a friendly farewell on his car horn.

The next couple of evenings we didn't go anywhere, just sat in the swing on our patio, holding hands and talking. I'm afraid I giggled a lot, especially when Doug tickled me on purpose with his beard.

On Friday morning Mama said, "Why don't you invite Doug over to dinner tonight, honey? To celebrate getting your cast off this afternoon?"

"Good idea," said my father, who hadn't yet left for the hospital. "I want to get better acquainted with the young man. Find out if he's really the man he seems, is worthy of Mags. Someday, say in five or six years, he may turn out to be our son-in-law."

"Talk about long-range planning," Mama said, laughing.

"Honestly, Father!"

"Never hurts to plan ahead, Mags. And Doug seems dependable, and as an engineer, especially with the doctorate he's aiming for, he should make a good living. But not now. You're not ready yet. Among other things you have to resolve this ballet thing. And for yourself. No one can do it for you. Not even me, I've found out the hard way."

"But I have resolved it. I'm going to be a dancer. Why should that keep me from marrying Doug, too? Now. If he asked me. It doesn't have to be Doug *or* ballet. It could be Doug *and* ballet."

"Maybe in five years, Mags, but not now. Ballet obsesses you now. In five years, you should either have succeeded in ballet, or accepted failure. Then, whether you're a dancer or not, you'll have the maturity, I hope, the ripeness to be a wife. Maybe Doug's."

"I could do both now."

"No. You're too tied up. You're both too tied up. You with ballet. Doug with engineering school for at least six more years. Both his school and your ballet career would be so demanding, so draining that neither of you would have anything left to give to a marriage."

"Oh, honestly, Father. We could, Doug and I, if we loved each other enough. But this is silly because we're not thinking of getting married. Ever."

I looked away from my father's steady appraising stare. His clinical gaze. I hoped I wasn't flushed, that I didn't sound too shrill. Because the way I felt about Doug these days, his kisses, his caresses—well, I couldn't get enough of him.

"We haven't got a future, Father. Doug and I are just for now."

"Well, you two seem mighty thick. Together every night. And he's good for you."

He paused, frowned at me. "You're not doing anything you shouldn't, are you, Maggie?"

"Oh, Father!"

"Because you're looking very well. Your eyes and skin are clear, shining. You're beginning to fill out. Look like a woman. Go get on the scales. You must have put on ten pounds."

"Ten pounds!"

I pushed away the scrambled eggs and toast Mama had set before me, got my crutch, and hobbled to the hall bathroom. He was nearly right. I had gained nine pounds, which for a person five feet, five inches makes a big difference. As for looking like a woman—yes, the full-length mirror showed more curve to my hips and fuller breasts. I would have to start dieting immediately if I was to get back my lithe slim body by the time my ankle grew strong enough to dance on.

Now, however, I did like seeing the twin swells of my breasts and the blue-white hollow that showed in the deep V of my T-shirt

So I made sure to wear a low-cut dress when Doug came to dinner that night. And I was able, although my ankle was weak and a little swollen, to meet him at the front door.

"Look, no cast! No crutches! I'm back among the walking!"

Doug lifted me, swung me around, and when he lowered me, lightly kissed my mouth.

I didn't know my father was right behind us. I blushed but Doug managed to give my father's hand a vigorous shake.

"Good to see you, Doug."

"Thank you, Dr. Adams."

"My name's Will. So call me Will. No need to be so formal. Some day I hope . . ."

"Excuse me, Will," Mama interrupted in the very nick of time while I squirmed with embarrassment. "I need you out here to turn the ice cream freezer."

When my father disappeared into the kitchen, Doug looped an arm around me and pressed his lips into my hair. He laughed at my red face.

"It's nice to be welcomed by your father. He didn't used to be so keen about me hanging around his pretty little daughter."

"Well, he's impressed by the future Ph.D. And he doesn't know about our no-tomorrows game, that our friendship is only for now. He thinks we have a future together and that your intentions are honorable, say in five or six years."

Brushing my hair off my forehead, smiling into my face, Doug said gently, "But they are honorable, Mag. They're honorable now."

"What are you talking about? In less than two weeks, you go to MIT and I get a job and try to go back to ballet. So what's this about honorable intentions?"

"I mean, Mag, that for these few beautiful weeks my intentions are honorable because I'm an honorable man. But honorable is not the same as permanent."

"This all sounds stupid. Like some sort of word game. Scrabble, maybe, which I hate."

Annoyed, I turned away from him so sharply that a pain shot from my left ankle, up my leg, clear to the hip. I cried out and limped to a sofa. Doug went down on his knees to rub my ankle.

"Sorry, Mag. Sorry."

Having heard me cry out, my father rushed in, brushed Doug aside, and with careful hands probed along the tendon.

"What were you trying to do, a damned *fouetté*?"

He rhymed the French ballet term with the English word "net." On purpose, I think, because he did study French when he was an undergraduate, after all.

"If I had had my way, you would still be wearing that cast for another week. Your ankle seems all right, though, but I want you to use your crutches, especially in the evening when your foot gets tired."

Thanks to Mama, dinner was delicious and she guided the conversation safely to engineering and medicine. And, happily, just as she was serving the homemade raspberry ice cream, my father's exchange phoned and he had to go out on a call.

127

All evening, Doug seemed especially tender, helped me to the patio door, lifted me down the steps, carried me to the swing. While we talked there, he stroked my hand and every once in a while lifted it to his chin to tickle it with his beard or to press a kiss against my palm. But we didn't really do any kissing until I walked with him to his car to say good night. Then he tilted up my face and caressed my mouth with his while I gave back kiss for kiss.

"Oh, Mag. Mag."

But he pulled away.

"Doug, what's the matter? What is it?"

"Nothing. You're just so sweet. But our friendship is only for now. And I told you I'm an honorable man. I'll phone you in the morning."

He did and we spent the next evening at the movies again. One night we drove to the city for dinner and a play. We spent a couple of evenings just watching TV at my house. But we never, never went where we were really alone. So our second week passed as quickly and uneventfully as the first.

Then he invited me to spend the Labor Day weekend sailing with his mother and some cousins on his uncle's thirty-four-foot sailboat. Maybe we would finally have some time alone.

Chapter Sixteen

What a laugh, expecting to have a few minutes alone on a sailboat—even one thirty-four feet long! There were always people. Doug and I could not talk, could hardly hold hands without someone bothering us. It was usually his two cousins—whose mother had made some excuse for not coming along. But after five minutes aboard, I suspected her real reason was to get away from those awful brats!

In her sister-in-law's absence, Doug's mother was in charge of the galley, while Doug and his cousins, aged nine and ten, took turns crewing. His Uncle Brian stayed at the wheel.

Early in the afternoon before the wind rose, we used the auxiliary motor to head out of the marina and up the bay. I sat on the padded bench of the cockpit and watched the boat's lacy wake, the blue hills sliding past, the huge steel network of the Oakland Bay Bridge, and San Francisco's abruptly soaring skyline.

Most of all, I admired Doug, naked to the waist, tanned, thin, but with wide-spreading shoulders. I saw him hoist the mainsail, then the jib, while his cousins capered underfoot like half-grown puppies. He returned to the cockpit to be near me, but every time Uncle Brian shouted, "Ready about! Hard alee!" Doug had to tighten one of the two ropes that controlled the front sail and loosen the second.

"Sheet, Mag," he whispered, smiling. "They're called sheets. For heaven's sake, don't let my uncle or cousins, particularly not those two brats, hear you call the jib sheets ropes."

He sneaked an arm around my waist, but there were the two boys, grinning beside us.

"Oh, lovey dovey!"

"Kiss her, Doug. Why'n't you kiss her?"

"Ferchrissake," yelled Doug's uncle from the rear of the cockpit. "Can't someone trim the jib? Stop it luffing. Pull in the sheet, can't you? Donny—Ted—somebody!"

Doug took a couple of turns of the sheet but the front sail kept flapping.

"Dammit, Doug, your girl friend's not going to wash overboard if you leave her for a second. So get up there and adjust the jib leads on their tracks. What do you think this is, the Love Boat?"

Doug climbed forward and, with his cousins romping at his heels, adjusted whatever it was his uncle wanted adjusted. He returned alone, having left the boys scuffling on the foredeck like colts saddled with orange life jackets.

We huddled together for a few minutes with his lips in my blowing hair. And then, up from the cabin came his mother bringing foul-weather jackets for Doug and his uncle.

"It's sure to get wet soon," she said.

After passing around crackers, smoked clams, and sodas, she sat down opposite us. Her face had the same strong bone structure as Doug's, her speech a slight Swedish accent.

"Isn't this delightful? So restful. And Douglas needs rest. Do you know, Maggie, that he will be putting in at least six years of hard work at MIT? He'll have no time then for sailing or frivolity."

Doug squeezed my hand and winked.

"Just label me 'grind'!"

"It's nothing to joke about, Douglas."

"No, Mother."

"And, Maggie dear, that pretty white skin of yours is getting all burned. Come down to the cabin and I'll put suntan oil on it."

"Thanks, Mrs. Anderson, but my father gave me some sunblock. You know, I have this stupid skin that goes with red hair."

"Then, for goodness sake, you'd better use your lotion before you burn to a crisp. And didn't you bring along a long-sleeved shirt? Well, put it on. And tie something around your hair. It's sure to get cold and windy as soon as we come out from behind San Francisco."

It did. I was still in the cabin putting on sunblock and a sweat shirt when the boat staggered, groaned, and began rolling. I climbed back to the cockpit and found the day completely changed. Coming out from behind the shelter of the hills and skyscrapers of the City, we were hit by wind, fog, and tide pouring through the Golden Gate. Uncle Brian called it the slot.

Around us the bay was dark green, white-capped, and choppy. On the cliffs out beyond the great bridge fog horns moaned. The sun, without warmth now, ducked in and out of the long roll of fog nosing in from the ocean.

I had only just stuck my head out of the cabin when cold spray hit the foredeck and slapped me hard, soaking my hair, the scarf I had tied around it, and my sweat shirt. I shuddered but the two awful cousins practically split their sides laughing and Uncle Brian shouted, "Welcome to sailing, Maggie!"

The next minute a gust threw the boat over to one side and bounced it along with the railing underwater. Doug pulled me close beside him on the high side of the slanting cockpit. I had to brace my feet against the opposite bench to keep from sliding into the angry green water.

"It's okay, Mag. We're not going to capsize or anything. This is called heeling."

His arm around me felt warm and comforting, but from the cabin his mother called, "Maggie, come back down here. You're soaking wet."

I pretended not to hear, and so did Doug. Soon, however, I wished I had done as she asked.

"The goddamned main's got to be reefed," bellowed Uncle Brian. "Get up there, Doug, and do it."

"I don't think I remember how."

"Ferchrissake, I showed you the last time you crossed the slot with me. I don't trust you at the helm while we're here in the middle of it, so I can't do the reefing myself. Get up there while I turn her into the wind. No, don't take Donny or Ted. They're no help. Take your girl friend. Put her to work."

I looked wild-eyed at Doug, but he smiled, strapped life jackets on both of us, and pulled me to my feet.

"Don't worry, Mag. You'll be okay. Reefing just means to shorten the mainsail so that the boat will be easier to handle in the wind. Won't heel so much."

Spray and waves washed over us while we climbed across the slippery slanting boat to the base of the great white wing of a sail. From behind the wheel, Doug's uncle shouted instructions.

"No, goddammit! Have your girl friend lower the sail while you reef. Not that goddamned halyard, sweetie. That's the jib halyard. The one on the starboard side, ferchrissake! Okay. Okay. Thata girl. Now cleat it. Cleat it, I said, sweetie! Fasten it around the goddamned cleat, ferchrissake!"

132

I wound the rope around what looked like a double hook, then waded back along the deck to wrestle with the loosened part of the sail while Doug tied it to the boom. The boat settled on its keel so that the cockpit was less vertical when we returned.

Wet and shivering, I leaned against Doug until his mother called us down into the cabin. There she handed us each a cup of hot soup. We drank it gratefully, hanging onto the chart table.

"You did fine, Mag," Doug said. "You really did. And don't mind Uncle Brian. He's actually a gentle soul, but sailing changes him into something of a Captain Bligh. As a matter of fact, every man I've ever sailed with is about as bad."

At five o'clock, we motored into the Berkeley marina where we planned to spend the night in a guest slip. During the docking, Uncle Brian cussed out one of the cousins for not cleating the bowline properly. At least Doug's uncle handed out his reprimands impartially!

After supper around the table in the main cabin, Doug and I offered to clean up.

"Oh, no, thanks," his mother said. "You're tired, Douglas. Why don't you rest awhile? Or, I know, you can take the boys on that walk they've been begging for. Maggie can stay and help me."

"Yes. Take us, Doug."

"We can't get out the security gate without the key, Doug."

"And Dad won't trust us with it."

Uncle Brian, poring over charts of the bay and planning tomorrow's adventure, tossed Doug the key.

"Here. Take them out of here. Give us a little peace and quiet."

When they returned, the boys fortunately decided to

stay on the dock to hunt for the crayfish they imagined were hiding among the pilings. Uncle Brian still sat at his chart table and Mrs. Anderson was in the head. Doug crept up to the triangular front cabin which I had to share with his mother. I was already in my sleeping bag.

"I came to tuck you in," he whispered so that his mother couldn't hear through the thin partition.

He sat down beside me.

"I'm so glad you're here, Mag. So glad."

He bent to kiss me good night just as his mother came out from the head. A long gray-blond braid hung down the back of her flannel nightgown.

"Douglas, dear, do let Maggie have a little privacy. The front cabin is out-of-bounds for men, you know."

And she shooed him into the main cabin to bunk with his cousins and uncle.

The next morning we motored out of the Berkeley marina just as the fog was lifting. Doug raised the sails, this time with my help. We remained on the foredeck, whispering, fingers interlaced. Milder this morning, the wind felt cool in our faces. The emerald water lapped around us. Marin County and various islands rose blue from the blue-green bay. The City shone like a mirage, a miracle of white sculptures. Peace. So peaceful. Doug and I kissed. But the two brats crept up behind us.

"Boy, oh, boy! Here they are, making out like crazy!"

Doug slammed a powerful backhand at them, and they retreated, squealing and yelling, along the slippery deck.

The only moment we really spent alone the whole weekend was late that afternoon on Angel Island. After securing the boat to a pair of buoys as directed by their father, Donny and Ted rowed us ashore at Ayala Cove in the dinghy. They promptly romped off to harass the deer grazing on the lawn among the picnic tables.

"Come on, Mag. Quick. Up the slope."

Doug pulled me off the road and up a steep hillside covered with sparse dry grass. Almost at our feet skimmed a shimmering blue swallow.

"Oh, look, Doug. How quick. How graceful."

"Like you, Mag. Like you, honey," he said. His voice broke on the word "honey." It was the first time he had ever called me that. "Come here before they miss us."

He led me behind a thick low-growing toyon tree whose green berries would turn red in time for Christmas. Hidden there, we went into each others' arms.

"Oh, Mag. Mag."

We began kissing wildly, our mouths opening, twisting together. When we paused to breathe, he murmured into my neck.

"Mag, it's not working out like I planned. I'm falling in love."

"Me, too. Oh, me, too."

We began kissing again, but suddenly the little hyenas were on us, screaming and yelling and scrambling up the bank.

"Kissy. Kissy."

"Smooch. Smooch. Smooch."

Then in high falsetto, "Oh, darling, do it again!"

That night we stayed at Ayala Cove and the next day sailed home. Doug's mother was with us when we stopped in front of my house late Monday afternoon.

"It was nice having you along, Maggie," she said. I saw the firm line of her jaw against the car window. "It was restful—especially for Douglas, who will be so very busy studying once he gets to MIT. He won't have much time for girls and sailing, I'm afraid. Good-bye, Maggie. Do call me sometime."

"Thank you, Mrs. Anderson."

Following Doug, I slid out of the car on the driver's side and waited silently while he worked the key into the lock and opened the trunk. He took out my duffel and sleeping bags and started up the curve of lawn with them. I limped along behind him, unable to keep up with his long strides. My ankle was tired and aching and I still rocked with the motion of the boat.

On the porch, he set down my bags and turned and waited for me to catch up. He took my hands in his.

"Good-bye, Mag."

A catch in his voice made me look at him quickly. His Adam's apple jerked up and down like it used to when he was upset long ago in high school.

"I'm afraid this is really good-bye, Mag. It's better to say it now, end it now."

I died a little, I think. Turned cold. White, I suppose. Would have fainted if I were the type who fainted. I could hardly get out the question.

"Why?"

"It hasn't worked out, Mag. Our game. I like you too much. And there's no future for us together. None. With your ballet and my six more years of school. I've been thinking a lot all during the sail, especially at night in my bunk. Especially since Angel Island. The only thing to do is break it off now. Right now, even if I don't leave for another week."

His windburned face looked tense and long. He was nearly crying. And I was, I was really sobbing.

"But a week's a week. A week is something."

"It would only make it worse. Besides, the way I feel, things might happen if we were together all that time."

"I don't care. Let them happen."

"Trust me, Mag. Please trust me. This is best."

He turned quickly, but I went after him, grabbed his arm.

"You can't go like this. I'll phone you. I'll come over."

"No, Mag, don't."

"I will. I'm going to."

"Well, Mag, I won't be there. I'm quitting my job, and my mother and I are going away for a few days. Down to Carmel."

"What?"

Then I saw it all. I was so shocked I really did have to catch hold of a porch pillar. But also I was furious. A red film blurred my vision.

"So this is all her idea."

"No, Mag. Except that last night, after you were in bed, she reminded me of my promise to take her to Carmel before I went away. Because after you and I started seeing each other again, I didn't want to go down there, couldn't bear to be away from you."

"But she managed to persuade you."

"It's not like you think, Mag. She's a widow, yes, but she doesn't cling. She's been counting on this trip, though. And then, she's really right about it's not being fair to you, or to me, to keep this going another week."

"And you believed her."

"Because she's right. More right than she knows. She doesn't know how crazy I am about you."

"Don't worry, she knows."

"Mag, she's not like that. She just wants me to be happy."

"Oh, for God's sake, Doug."

"I'm not going to argue. Try to understand."

"All right. Then it's good-bye. Good-bye, good-bye, good-bye! Have a great time in Carmel! Have a great life!"

I whirled away from him and slammed into the house.

137

Chapter Seventeen

The next few days without Doug were empty, desolate. The loss of the apprenticeship had hurt my ego, but I felt his loss as much physically as emotionally. Besides missing his companionship, I longed for his warmth, his gentleness, his nearness.

I drifted around the house, my eyes swollen, a soggy handkerchief in my hand. Every once in a while I crumpled into a chair or onto my bed for another cry. When my father was home I could see him watching me while he pretended to read the newspaper or one of his journals.

"Come here, Mags," he said one morning, Thursday, I think. His tone was brisk, hearty—his bedside-manner voice. "Let me check that ankle and tendon of yours."

I slumped down on a sofa and plopped my left foot across his lap.

"Hmm. No swelling. Seems fine. I think maybe you can start doing a little *barre* work again. But very, very slowly. Ask McMichael for some exercises to strengthen your ankle. Then try a little stretching, bending, things you can do sitting down, or without putting much weight on your left foot. How does that sound, Mags?"

I knew he was being kind, wanted to help get my mind off Doug. Imagine my father suggesting I start ballet again! And I appreciated it, but I felt so empty, so limp, too limp even to dance.

"Thanks. Maybe I will."

"And, Maggie dear," Mama said, "why don't you go to McMichael's today? You may use my car. He still needs your help, you know."

"Besides, you don't want me moping around the house all day again! Why don't you just say it straight out?"

"Baby, I just want to help you. Go on down. Do a few easy exercises. It will be good for you."

So I went, answered the telephone, tried some foot exercises McMichael showed me, did some sit ups, worked on my turnout, bent my knees in a few *pliés*, even put up my left foot and slid it along the *barre*. But I felt listless and stiff, and when the kids started coming in, I really had to make an effort to smile.

Most of them were already in the studio when Joyce rushed in. Late for the eleven o'clock class, she headed straight toward the dressing room, but stopped when she saw me. I had phoned her about Doug going off to Carmel.

"Mag! How are you doing?"

I shrugged.

"This is not our summer, is it, Mag? And it may not be Lupe's either. She phoned me just as I was leaving the house. That's why I'm late. She said she had been trying to call you. She's getting married, Mag, marrying Eddy."

"Eddy? I thought she broke up with him."

"Yes, but now the wedding's on again. And she wants us to come. It's tomorrow night, the same night it was originally set for. She said she'd phone you here."

Joyce went off to dress and I dialed an old number I found for Lupe in McMichael's records, but it had been disconnected. In a little while though, she phoned me.

"Did Joyce tell you, *cariña*? Eddy and me, we're getting married, after all."

Her voice sounded strained and faint.

"Lupe, are you crying? What's wrong?"

"Oh, Maggie, I love him so much, but everything's awful!"

Then the idea jumped into my head that she had to get married, that she was pregnant. I mean, it was logical. First, she broke off the engagement even after the wedding date was set. And now, suddenly, she was marrying him after all. Because she was my best friend, I asked her straight out if she thought she was going to have a baby.

"Oh, no, *cariña*. It's not that. Eddy and me, we don't do nothing like that—we hardly make out at all. His church, our church, it believes you should wait, you know, till after the wedding."

"Then why are you crying? You love him and you're going to marry him."

"It's my family. They're Catholic, you know. And they say, if me and Eddy aren't married in the Church, meaning the Catholic Church, that we'll be living in sin. So they won't come to the wedding. Neither will Eddy's folks 'cause they're Catholic too."

"I'm really sorry, Lupe."

"What I wanted to say, Maggie, was that along with Paul, you and Joyce are my best friends. So I want you all at my wedding. But, of course, I can't invite Paul because of how Eddy feels about people who are, well, gay. And I know it's late to ask, but will you be a bridesmaid along with Joyce?"

"Sure, Lupe, of course. But, Lupe," I couldn't help asking, "what about ballet? Did Eddy finally agree to let you dance? Is that why you're marrying him?"

"Oh, no, *cariña*. I gave up dancing. I found out I couldn't stand not having Eddy. And since I couldn't have both . . ."

After we hung up, I stared out McMichael's green-tinted windows. Poor Lupe. Then I thought, a little hysterically, well, at least I didn't have to choose between ballet and Doug! At the moment, I had neither.

The rest of Thursday I cheered up a little, maybe because of coming down to McMichael's, maybe because of realizing that I really would dance again, or maybe because Lupe's troubles took my mind off my own.

And then Friday morning, just as I walked into McMichael's waiting room, the phone started ringing. It was Doug.

"Mag, I came back from Carmel. I had to. I left my mother there with friends. Can I see you right now? I don't blame you for being mad. I almost ruined everything."

When his orange sports car pulled up at McMichael's curb fifteen minutes later, I asked a mother of one of the students to take any phone calls. The next minute I was beside Doug in the bucket seat. Putting both arms around his waist, I pressed my face against the muscles of his upper arm.

"Don't cry, Mag. Oh, don't cry, honey. Everything's going to be all right."

He drove straight through town and up into the heavily wooded foothills. I leaned my cheek against his shoulder, fingered the round muscles of his arm, kissed the blue veins in the crook of his arm.

"Come on, Mag, take it easy. Look, it's prettier up here than ever."

I sat up to admire the twisted madrones he was pointing out. Round, smooth, orange, their limbs seemed almost human. They held bouquets of yellow and green leaves out over the crumbling asphalt road.

"I'll never forget our picnics up here, Mag. And how I

kissed you for the first time long ago when we were just kids."

That long-ago afternoon was cool, I remembered. It was later in the year than now. October. Maybe even November. A cold breeze had blown suddenly across the lake, spinning golden leaves in the birch tree above us, ruffling our picnic cloth, making me shiver, so he had taken me in his arms to warm me and to kiss me for the very first time.

"Of course, I remember, Doug. But I'm surprised you do. I thought you didn't want any yesterdays. Any tomorrows, either."

"That didn't work out, Mag. That's why I came back from Carmel. I've fallen in love and it's not just our old high school puppy love, either."

"Oh, me, too, Doug."

He shifted his car into second and turned into the park with its bald tawny hills opposite dark wooded slopes of conifers, oaks, and toyon trees. He started to circle down to the blue oblong of the lake where lines of parked cars shone in the sunlight.

"Why don't we go up there?" I asked, pointing to the road that twisted up to the highest dome. "There won't be as many people."

He smiled at me, gunned up the steep incline, and parked at the vista point. We looked down the rounded hills, golden brown this time of year, tawny, and scattered with the dark green ovals of giant oaks. We could see the whole wide valley, down which stretched, from San Francisco to San Jose, the flat blue bay.

Behind us, above the high spine of the coast range, spread the fog like a frothing ocean breaker, threatening to tumble over us and roll down into the valley. But we were the only people admiring all this. Doug's car was

143

alone at the vista point. Putting an arm around me, he lifted my face and lightly kissed me.

"Let's get the blanket out of the trunk, Mag, our old plaid blanket, and find a quiet place to talk about our future. Because we do have a future together, Mag. We have to have."

He took out the blanket that I remembered from all our earlier picnics. With it under one arm, and holding me by the hand—"because of your ankle, Mag"—he led me carefully down the steep grassy slope to a clump of fir trees that would screen us from the road.

"So we'll have a little privacy. So it won't be like that damned mob scene on my uncle's boat."

He gave me an apologetic smile and spread the blanket on the ground, flattening the high dry grass under it.

"What? No bratty cousins?"

"No, nobody, but you, me, and a few friendly cows minding their own business."

He pointed down the slope to where, beyond a narrow gully, a string of white-faced cattle paraded along a lower, perfectly rounded hill.

"We should have brought a picnic lunch, Mag, so it would be like old times."

"It is like old times. Besides, I'm not hungry. I'm just glad, really happy that you came back, that we're here."

Moving against him, I fastened my arm around his waist and reached up to kiss him. Laughing a little, he held me away from him and tickled my face with his beard.

"I want to talk about our future, Mag."

"All right, let's. I'm so glad we finally have a future after that silly here-and-now game of yours."

Giggling, I kissed him.

"No, Mag, I'm serious."

"So am I. And I'm crazy about you."

I went on kissing him until he gave up trying to talk and concentrated on our kisses. I began to feel dizzy, overwhelmed, soft. I opened my mouth to his tongue. I let him stroke and fondle me until suddenly, I heard a car stop above us at the vista point. I pulled away from him.

"Oh, Doug, we'd better stop. Someone will see us."

"Not way down here. Not behind these trees."

"They might come down. And I'd be so embarrassed. Please, Doug."

"Well, I suppose you're right, honey. So what I started to say, Mag, was that I love you and want you to come East with me. We can live together while I go to school. Or we can get married. Whatever you want. But I can't lose you."

He put his arms around me again.

"Oh, Doug, I'd love to, but I wonder . . . shouldn't we talk about it a little? Make plans or something?"

"We can work out the details later. Now, just say you'll come with me."

He began kissing me again, holding me, stroking me, until I could think only of wanting him, of loving him.

"Yes, Doug. Oh, yes. Yes, I'll come."

"And will you let me make love to you now? I heard the car pull away."

"Oh, Doug, I want to. But not here. Please. I'm afraid someone might come."

"Okay, honey. Later then?"

"Of course. I really want to."

Thinking what it would be like, I leaned against him. I watched the pale sky, looked at new needles greening the tips of the fir boughs, saw the fog start its slow cascade down the hillside. It was midafternoon before we folded the blanket and climbed arm-in-arm up the hill to his car.

On the twisting ride down from the park, I cuddled against him, burrowed my face into the deep hollow between his neck and shoulder.

"Tell me about Boston, Doug."

"We won't be living in Boston, Mag. MIT's in Cambridge, same as Harvard."

"I just mean, what'll we do back there?"

"Live together. Love each other. We'll be together in our own snug little place."

"Do you know where we'll live?"

"No, but I'll find us somewhere, and then you'll come later."

"Later! But I don't ever want to be away from you again, Doug. It's too terrible, too lonely. When we're not together, I'm nothing. I feel sort of like I'm amputated from you. Can't I go the same time you go?"

"Of course, honey. Oh, Mag, I love you so much!"

We came up to a stop sign at the bottom of the hill and he paused a long time to give me a long kiss. Behind us, a car honked.

When Doug drove on, he said, "I really want you to come with me right away. I only suggested waiting because I thought Sunday might be too soon for you to get ready."

"Sunday? Day after tomorrow?"

"I know it's awfully soon. But I have to get oriented and registered, find housing, see my counselor, all that stuff."

"It's just so soon, Doug!"

Pressed against him, I started feeling scared about the East, about what it would be like. I mean, I'd hardly been anywhere. I was born here and had lived all my life in the same house. Once, long ago, I visited New York when Papa attended a medical conference there. And my parents took me with them to Italy and Spain when I was ten.

But I had only been away from them once in my entire life: three years ago when I went to a Ballet Association Festival in southern California. What would it be like to live far away on the East Coast? But I knew what life without Doug was like!

I kept one hand on his forearm, feeling the muscles roll when he shifted gears. We were completely out of the foothills now and gliding down into the sloping well-groomed suburb where I lived.

"Doug, I'm a little worried."

"Don't be, honey. Remember, we'll be together."

"Not all the time. You'll be in school a lot. And studying. My father says graduate school is really hard. Also, what about my ballet?"

"Mag, everything will work out. First, your ankle has to heal. But there are ballet schools in Boston. And maybe you can get a job."

"In a ballet school?"

"Maybe, or even in a ballet company. Only that would keep you away from me a lot, wouldn't it?"

When he swung his car into our driveway, I invited him to a late lunch, but he said he had packing to do.

"And I should phone my mother down in Carmel and tell her about us."

He promised to come to dinner, though, so that we could break the news to my parents. He also said he would go with me to Lupe's wedding.

"And, Mag, with my mother in Carmel, we can spend the night at my house afterwards."

His suggestion really bothered me. I mean, I loved him and wanted to make love. But I wanted it to happen naturally, beautifully, unplanned. I hated the idea of sneaking into his house while his mother was away.

147

"What would I tell my parents?"

"I don't know. The truth."

"I couldn't."

"Then say you're spending the night with a girl friend, with Joyce. She's coming to Lupe's wedding, isn't she? Anyway, think about it."

From the time Doug's car backed out of the driveway until he drove in again later, I thought about it. And about going East. I also wondered why I was making such a big deal about these decisions when I loved Doug, was crazy about him.

I couldn't sit still, couldn't eat the yogurt I took out of the refrigerator. In my room, I stared at all my books and records, wondering which ones to take. I dragged out a suitcase and filled it with underwear, nightgowns, and ballet tights. The next minute, though, I threw everything back into my dresser.

Once I paused beside my canary's cage and watched his yellow throat bubble out with song. Oh, how could I leave Poppy? But how could I take him? Finally, I gave up, filled the tub with Mama's bubble bath, and sank into mountains of rustling lilac-scented foam.

When Doug returned, I met him wearing low-heeled sandals, pronounced 'sensible' by Papa, and my green silk dress. It was the only long one I had, the only suitable one to wear as Lupe's bridesmaid. After *Serpent*, Mama had mended the torn hem, stitched up the split seam at the waist, and sent the dress to the cleaners.

"You look so beautiful," Doug said, hugging me. "Did you tell them?"

I shook my head. He took my hand and pulled me, re-sisting, to where my father sat reading.

"Coward. We'll tell him now."

"Wait, Doug. It would make dinner awful. I'll tell them myself tomorrow."

"Promise?"

"Promise."

Dinner was rushed. Halfway through the herbed chicken over rice, my father received an emergency call from the hospital. Then Doug and I couldn't wait for dessert because I wanted to get to the church in plenty of time to help Lupe. I was sure she would really need me.

Chapter Eighteen

After driving around the old part of town for fifteen minutes, Doug and I finally located Eddy's church in a storefront between a secondhand furniture shop and a Mexican bakery. The other stores in the block sat vacant. Painted white, their windows resembled eyes blinded by cataracts.

An opaque whitewash also covered the windows of the church, but they did not seem sightless like their neighbors. Ringed by poster-painted yellow daisies and red gladiolas, black letters on the glass proclaimed: "¡*Jesús Salva!*" An English translation followed: "Jesus Saves!"

Doug parked his car around the corner and, holding hands, we walked back to Eddy's church. I hesitated at the front door, but Doug reached around me to open it. We seemed to be the first arrivals.

Inside yawned a room the size of a warehouse or, maybe, an unset stage. Its floor was rough concrete. Fluorescent ceiling tubes shed a brilliance as harsh as the working lights in a theatre. Six rows of folding metal chairs formed semicircles around a platform of unpainted plywood, apparently hastily nailed together. To its right stood an upright piano stained dark brown. Painted on the plaster wall behind the platform loomed a thick black cross. Around it, someone had dabbed more of the same daisies and gladiolas that decorated the front windows.

Although I saw nobody, I heard voices somewhere toward the back. Soon a door, which I hadn't noticed, opened and through it came two middle-aged Mexican women in shapeless black dresses. Their hair lay down their backs in thick single braids.

Without looking at us, they solemnly approached the platform. On it, one woman spread the small white rug she carried. The other placed her basket of white gladiolas there too. Setting the stage for Lupe's wedding? I held tighter to Doug's hand and to the shawl around my shoulders.

Now the women, having completed what seemed for them a solemn ritual, nodded to us. Their smiles revealed mouthfuls of decayed and gold-filled teeth. Instead of saying Hello or Good evening, they greeted us with, "Praise the Lord!"

"Are you friends of Lupe?" one woman asked. "She's dressing but said to go back. Not the *señor*, of course."

"Do you mind, Doug?" I asked.

"No, go ahead. I'll sit here and see how it's done. For future reference, of course."

I giggled but didn't enjoy his teasing as much as usual. I would be glad when this wedding was over and we were out of this awful place.

Leaving Doug studying the mural of black cross and flowers, I followed the Mexican women. They led me past a kitchen and into a large bathroom where Lupe stood in front of a small square mirror. Joyce worked behind her, fastening a short net veil to her hair. Lupe and I ran into each other's arms.

"Maggie. *Cariña*. I'm so glad you're here."

"Listen, you two, no tears. Mag, I just stopped her crying. And now you come. It's a good thing these people don't believe in makeup or Lupe's face would be one smeary mess."

I backed away so that Joyce could finish dressing Lupe. She looked tinier than ever, and very thin, in a floor-length white gown with a fitted bodice, long tight sleeves, and a high collar. I wondered where the dress came from. Lupe had no money and certainly her family, if they refused even to come to the wedding, wouldn't provide a gown. I asked her about the dress.

"A sister—all the women here are sisters—is letting me use it. The people in this church are good. Really kind, you know."

"Then things can't be so awfully bad, Lupe," Joyce said.

"Oh, no. Things aren't bad at all. The women, they brought all kinds of Mexican food. That's how come all those pots and casseroles are there in the kitchen. After the wedding the sisters are going to give a big supper. Everybody's invited."

"It's sort of a religious community then," Joyce said, "like the early Christians."

"Oh, yes, they're really good people. But I just want my family here. I love Eddy, but I'm awful lonely for my mother and sisters."

Out in the hall a woman called in a singsong voice, almost a chant, "Lupe? Guadalupe? Praise the Lord, little sister. Brother Edwardo sends his love and expresses his great joy that today you will become his bride. Joyfully, he asks if you are ready to come forward to marry him in the presence of the Lord and our Christian brotherhood. Praise the Lord!"

Joyce and I backed away, leaving Lupe wide-eyed, swaying in the middle of the bathroom. I remembered three years ago when she fainted just before Joyce's *Golden Shoes* ballet. Now she reached out to us.

"I'm so scared, *cariña*, Joyce."

We each took one of her hands. I dabbed at her tears with a piece of Kleenex.

"Listen, Lupe, it's Eddy you're marrying," Joyce said. "You love each other."

"Yes, I know. I know I love Eddy. But I want my mother, *mi mamá. Por dios, dónde está?*"

Her tears fell faster than I could wipe them away. In my hand, hers lay damp and cold. Mine was cold too.

"*Madre mía*, I want my St. Christopher. I need it," Lupe said. "But Eddy said no."

"That seems little enough to ask. Where is it? I'll get it," Joyce said.

"In my purse on the shelf. In the gold box."

Opening the purse, Joyce took out Lupe's medal, fastened the chain around her neck, and dropped the small gold oval down the inside of the wedding dress.

"There. Nobody will know the difference. And, Lupe, listen, it's your decision. If you want Eddy, now is the time to marry him. If you don't, now is the time to say so."

"Oh, I do want him. Only . . ."

"Then pull yourself together, girl. You too, Mag. You're not helping at all!"

Joyce opened the door and we stood back to let Lupe leave, but she didn't go. Standing there, she reached down the front of her dress and yanked out the St. Christopher, breaking its chain. For a moment, she held the medal across her palms, across her graceful dancer's hands. Then she put it into mine.

"Keep it, *cariña*, to remember me by. I'm marrying Eddy so I got to do what he says."

"Everything?"

I shouldn't have asked, but I had to. I meant dancing, of course, but I could tell by the look she gave me from wide, tear-filled eyes, that for her, everything really meant everything. Not only ballet, but religion, friends, family. Especially her *mamá*.

"Yes, everything. Eddy says a good wife obeys her husband same as a good man obeys the Lord. And 'cause I love Eddy so much and am marrying him, I got to do everything he says."

Lowering her veil, she left the bathroom.

"Praise the Lord," I heard her whisper to the group of women outside. I closed my fingers over the St. Christopher and went with Joyce out into the drafty main room.

With efficient hands, one of the sisters moved us into the bridal procession: Joyce first, then me, and finally Lupe on the arm of a gray-haired, crew-cut brother who was substituting for her absent father. The same hands passed around small nosegays of daisies and gladiolas, obviously picked from backyards and pressed through the middle of paper doilies. My flowers were yellow, so were Joyce's, but Lupe's were pure virginal white.

When the piano began the wedding march, it was the familiar "Here Comes the Bride!" thumped out as regularly as drum beats. Joyce led, with me following like a sleepwalker, and Lupe behind, across the concrete floor, down the aisle between the folding chairs now dark with people. I didn't see Doug. I didn't see anybody. For me, the people blended together into one dark mass.

The pastor waited in front of the cross for the wedding party to come to him.

"Who gives this woman in marriage?" he asked.

"I do," said the stand-in for Lupe's father. He moved away, leaving her alone, a tiny white-veiled child.

Then for the first time I saw Eddy. He stepped up to her, not smiling for once. He was almost frowning. He wore a plain white shirt and a double-breasted black suit, not one of those effeminate blue or magenta wedding costumes for men.

The pastor began saying prayers, but for me, the words wove together into a meaningless hum, and in the intervals, as regular as drumbeats, came the shout from the people: "Praise the Lord!"

The pastor said, "You may join hands."

I saw Lupe's hand go into Eddy's and I remembered the weight of Armando's, Huitzilopochtli's, on mine. Joyce put her arm around my waist.

"You're shivering, Mag. Are you cold?"

"Yes. No. I don't know. Maybe I'm catching something."

"It is drafty in here. Better sit down."

Someone moved to give me a chair, where I sat, not hearing, only staring at Lupe's hand in Eddy's. After a while, gold rings were pushed onto their fingers, and then came the words: "Will you love, honor, and obey . . . ?" Obey! Dear God, obey!

"I will," Lupe said.

The pastor blessed the pair.

"And now in the presence of the Lord and this assembly, I pronounce you husband and wife."

"Praise the Lord!" said the people around me.

Eddy lifted Lupe's short veil to reveal her smiling, tear-tracked face. He leaned to kiss her but was stopped by a moan, then a shriek. Running down the aisle came a heavy, dark-shawled woman. She pulled Lupe away from the startled bridegroom.

"*Mi hija. Mi pobre hijita!*"

I recognized Lupe's mother and remembered that, on the night that Lupe collapsed with anorexia, her mother had also come. I could still see her, sitting in the middle of the dressing room floor three years ago, rocking her poor little daughter, her *pobre hijita*.

156

Tonight, behind Lupe's mother came Tonie, an older sister.

"*Mamá!*" Tonie cried. "Lupe, forgive us. We went out, telling Papa we were going to the store. And Mama promised to be quiet, to sit way at the back. Let's go *Mamá. Ya nos vamos.*"

But the mother refused to release her daughter. I saw fresh tears start down Lupe's face.

"*Tu viniste, Mamá,*" Lupe said and continued in Spanish. Joyce translated softly for me. "You came, Mama. You came. Thank you. I love you. I'll always love you. But now Eddy is my husband. And you must go back with Tonie."

The mother clung, however, until Tonie, Joyce, and some of the churchwomen finally managed to ease her up the aisle and out the front door. Still seated, I watched Lupe and Eddy exchange their bridal kiss.

"Great wedding!" Doug said, coming to find me. He pulled me to my feet and shook hands with Joyce. She had returned to find out how I was feeling.

"What was so great?" I asked. "I hated it. The whole ceremony. Lupe promising to obey. The way he clutched her hand. Reminded me of *Serpent.*"

"*Serpent*? Mag, you're crazy!" Joyce said. "They were just holding hands like couples do at every wedding."

"Maybe I just hate weddings then."

"Listen, Mag. What's wrong with you?" Joyce asked. "Lupe adores Eddy and knows exactly what she's getting into. She's going to be fine. It's you I'm worried about. Come on, let's go have some of that great Mexican food."

"No, I'm not hungry. I just want to get out of here. Besides we ate just before we came."

Joyce gave me a long look.

"Well, okay. But relax. Take care of her, Doug."

157

Chapter Nineteen

Around the corner from the church, Doug put me in the car and then climbed into the driver's seat. But instead of turning on the ignition, he sat and looked at me.

"Well, Mag, feeling better now? My house or yours?"

I didn't answer. I stayed where I was, didn't slide over close to him. In my hand Lupe's St. Christopher had grown warm and comforting.

A dozen feet ahead of Doug's car a street lamp showered milky light down on a littered sidewalk, on a battered pickup truck, on a long shiny automobile bearing the only manufacturer's trademark that I could recognize: "V" for Cadillac.

"If I had a Cadillac, I wouldn't park it in this awful neighborhood," I said, facing straight ahead but aware, very aware of Doug and his quiet eyes studying me.

"Want to talk about it, Mag?"

"Oh, Doug. It was just so awful, so awful, seeing Lupe marry Eddy."

Doug's arms reached out for me and I went into them. He held me quietly where I could feel his regular breathing, up and down, up and down, comforting me, not like a boyfriend, not like a lover with exploring hands. More like a father, like Papa used to hold me when I was little and scared of the dark. Above my head, Doug's breath came warm and moist into my hair.

"What did you think was so awful about the wedding? I thought it was interesting."

"Interesting!" I shuddered. "First of all, that awful place. Drafty and cold. A big empty warehouse. Everything jammed into one corner. And all the people tottering around in dark clothes. 'Praise the Lord!' 'Praise the Lord!'"

"Mag, they weren't all in dark clothes. And they didn't totter. A lot of them were young, our age. Eddy's best man, for instance."

"Did he have a best man? I didn't notice. All I saw was Eddy hanging onto Lupe's hand, and how sad she looked."

"A pretty distorted view, I'd say."

"No. She was sad. She was crying all the time. All the way through the ceremony."

"Lots of brides cry."

"Not like that, Doug."

"Well, she didn't have to marry him. She could have said no."

"She did once. But then she went back. She loves him much too much to see what he really is."

"To see what you think he is."

"What he is: demanding. Intolerant. Insensitive. A smiling bully. And she's given up everything for him."

Doug brushed a lock of hair away from my face and looked at me straight.

"I'm getting the message that this has something to do with us."

I looked away.

"Mag, I'm not asking you to give up everything. Nothing, really. We'll be in Massachusetts, but that's not another planet. And your parents like me. They could visit us and you could visit them."

"They think we're too young and too busy to make a marriage work. Especially Papa."

"Parents always do. Especially fathers."

"What about mothers? What did yours say?"

"I haven't told her yet. She'll agree with your parents, though. But none of them know how much we love each other. Besides, if I told her now she would rush straight home from Carmel. And I don't want that. I want you to spend the night with me."

He lowered his face to mine and began kissing the inner corners of my eyes. I rolled my face aside.

"Doug, listen. No, I mean it. Aren't you asking me to give up ballet, like Eddy asked Lupe?"

"So that's it. No, Mag, you can keep dancing till you're eighty-five. One-hundred-and-five, if you want to."

"But you said you didn't want me to join the Boston Ballet. You said it would take too much of my time, take me away from you, or something like that."

"It would. It probably would. You get so carried away. But I didn't say you couldn't dance with the Boston Ballet, if they accepted you."

"If they accepted me. If. And you think they won't. Just like my father, you think they won't. Just because I didn't get an apprenticeship with City Ballet."

"Mag, you're putting words into my mouth. I love you. I want you. So anything you do is okay with me."

"Really?"

"Yes."

Putting my arms around his neck, I began kissing him. He responded, not like a father anymore. I slid into a delicious dizziness until suddenly we were shocked apart by someone banging on the car door. Looking out my side, I gave a little scream. For, framed in the window, grinned a dark Mexican face with a long hawk nose and teeth

161

gleaming white in the shine of the street lamp. I couldn't make out the rest of the face, but I shuddered.

"Jesus," Doug muttered and reached to open the door on his side. I grabbed his arm.

"No. Don't get out. He looks like, oh, Doug, he reminds me of that terrible Aztec god."

"Relax, Mag. It's some punk wanting his stupid little joke. But it's no joke. And it was dumb of me to park here. Let's get going."

Doug started the motor and drove me straight to my house. When he stopped at the curb, I was still shaking.

"Sorry about what happened, Mag. I guess you wanted to come home, not to my house, didn't you? Well, maybe it's better that we don't start out by deceiving our parents. We'll have plenty of nights together later."

I nodded, relieved but also disappointed. At the front door he kissed me.

"Get a good night's sleep, honey. I'll come in the morning to talk things over when you're calmer."

But I didn't get a good night's sleep. Like the princess in the fairytale, I couldn't relax, couldn't get comfortable. But my magic pea wasn't round and green and buried under dozens of mattresses. Mine was some terrible drawn-out nightmare.

When I woke up in the morning, I remembered almost nothing about it except cold green waves washing over me and a confusion of men, one changing into another: Huitzilopochtli, Armando, Eddy, and, I think, Doug and Quetzalcoatl. All shouted orders at me. "Cleat the halyard, ferchrissake. Reef the main!"

It was nearly ten o'clock when I wandered into the kitchen, barefooted, wearing a white nightgown, and still haunted by the nightmare. My parents looked up from their breakfast. How could I tell them about going East with Doug?

Mama smiled.

"Well, dear, how was the wedding?"

"Awful, Mama. I don't want to talk about it."

"Sorry I asked."

I saw Papa eye me, but for once, he made no comment. I sat down at my place and stared at the waiting glass of orange juice.

"Doug's coming over," I said.

"So what else is new?" Papa asked, but he smiled. "I like Doug. Someday, I hope you marry a man like him, Mags."

There. He had given me my opening, but I chickened out. Then Doug was at the door.

"Go put on a robe," my father said. "I hope you're not planning to let him in, wearing only a nightgown."

"Oh, Father!"

"Honestly, Will. It's perfectly modest, covers far more than her bathing suits or leotards. Don't be so Victorian."

"Well, I don't like it."

I left them arguing and ducked out onto the front porch and into Doug's arms. Oh, he was so beautiful! That long lean body widening at the shoulders. The thatch of straw-colored hair, backlighted by the morning sun. The thin tan face, the dark blue eyes, and the smile, pink and friendly in the middle of his soft red beard. I reached my mouth up for a long kiss.

"Will I get kissed like that every morning?" he asked, putting his arm around me, pushing open the screen door. "What did your parents say?"

"I haven't told them yet."

We faced each other in the entrance hall. I felt the tiles chilling my bare feet. His hands cupped my shoulders, his eyes peered into mine, as if he were trying to read them.

"Have you changed your mind then about going East?"

I watched my toes curling on the tiles.

"I don't know."

"What's wrong, Mag? Don't you love me?"

I looked up quickly. "Oh, I do love you."

"Then why haven't you told them? Why do you keep putting it off?"

"I'm just so mixed up."

I turned away from him and went into the living room. Looking out, I saw the sun and shade patterns moving under the oak trees. Doug followed me, stood behind me, stroked my bare arms up and down, slid aside one lace shoulder strap to kiss my skin beneath it.

"What are you afraid of, honey?"

"Everything, I guess. Mainly, not being allowed to dance. Because I couldn't give up ballet like Lupe did."

His arms went around me.

"Mag, I've told you, you don't have to give up ballet. You can dance in Boston. We've already talked about that. I thought it was settled. Clear. Don't you believe me?"

"I guess not."

"But why?"

"I don't know. I guess I remember how you felt about it in high school, how you really feel about it now. And I'm afraid."

We were silent, standing together, me a little in front of him, his hands playing in my hair.

"I'll say it again. I'll say it a hundred times. You can dance in Boston. You can dance in Boston."

I looked at him. I did love him. He was Doug, not that awful Eddy! And a nightmare was only a dream. Besides, don't parents always think you're too young, too inexperienced? And Doug did keep promising I could dance. So what was I afraid of? I reached my arms around his waist.

"All right, Doug. Let's go tell them."

As he bent to kiss me, I heard the telephone ringing.

"Maggie, it's for you," Mama called from the kitchen.

"Can't I phone them back?"

"It's Madame Martina from City Ballet."

A shiver ran through me, like the freezing hot touch of dry ice. Maybe she wanted to inquire about my ankle or even ask if I would teach a beginning technique class next fall. But it was neither.

"Maggie, maybe you already know that Lupe Herrera got married and has given up her apprenticeship? I've been asked to offer it to you."

Dear God!

And here came Doug into the kitchen, silhouetted against the light from the patio. He ducked his head to avoid the door frame. Mama stood watching me, holding a plate and cup she was about to put into the dishwasher. Papa looked up from his newspaper.

"Maggie, are you still there?" Martina asked.

"Yes."

"I know it's sudden, dear. And, of course, you should have had it all along. But we'll soon be getting into *Nutcracker* rehearsals so we need to know right away. Will you accept the apprenticeship?"

I croaked out the word. "Yes."

"Good. I'm so glad. I hoped you would. Report Monday then for Company class. And, I'm sure, this will be a great opportunity for you, a whole new beginning."

I hung up the phone.

"What was that all about?" Papa asked.

"Lupe's apprenticeship. The Company gave it to me."

"Well, I'll be damned. Congratulations. So you finally got what you wanted, Mags. My daughter, the ballet dancer."

I didn't look at Doug who stood in the bright doorway. He didn't say anything—maybe sensing some problem. Neither did Mama.

Finally, she said, "Maggie, why don't you and Doug go out on the patio? It's nice out there."

"That's all right, Mrs. Adams. I have packing to do. I'm leaving tomorrow. I just came to say good-bye and to bring Maggie something she left in my car."

At arm's length, he dangled Lupe's St. Christopher. I took it without looking at him.

"Good-bye, Mrs. Adams," he said, pulling away when she reached to kiss him. "Good-bye, Dr. Adams." He did shake the hand Papa offered. Then he shot me a look from steel-blue eyes. "Good-bye, Maggie. Let me know if your Company ever visits Boston. I might come see you dance."

He turned and walked out of the kitchen.

"Doug!"

I ran after him. "Doug, I'm sorry. It's not that I don't love you."

He kept on walking out of the house, across the porch, down the sweep of front lawn. I went after him.

"Doug. This isn't the end. I'll write to you. Maybe we'll see each other next summer."

On the far side of his car, he paused and looked across the orange top that shone golden in the sunlight. He waited until I was opposite. I could see the shine of tears in his eyes.

"Why, Mag? Tell me, why? Don't you love me enough?"

I shook my head, felt tears of my own.

"I don't know. Really I don't. I'm just not ready yet, I guess."

"Well, at least my mother would be relieved. If she

knew. Which she won't. Because it hurts too much to talk about. But, later, maybe I'll write you, Mag. Maybe not. I really don't know yet. Well, good-bye."

Folding his long body into the little car, he pulled away from the curb and burned rubber all the way to the stop sign. There his brake lights winked briefly before he went around the corner.

Then, when he had gone, was completely out of sight, I heard the brief toot-toot of his car horn. Oh, Doug! Doug! Passing slowly under the great tent of the oak tree, I walked back to the house with his familiar farewell signal still sounding in my ears.

KAREN STRICKLER DEAN has been a balleto-
mane for more than forty years. She studied with
Bronislava and Irina Nijinska in Los Angeles and
with the San Francisco Ballet School. In her novels
for young readers, she hopes to convey the excitement of ballet while showing a realistic portrait of a
dancer's world.

Karen Strickler Dean has been writing since she
was nine years old and has written a number of arti-
cles and short stories for magazines and educational
publications. Presently a school teacher for children
with learning disabilities, she lives in Palo Alto,
California, with her husband. They have four
grown children.

FLARE ORIGINAL NOVELS
FOR YOUNG ADULTS
By
KAREN STRICKLER DEAN

Ms. Dean, a former dancer, conveys the excitement and discipline of the dance world to her readers.

MAGGIE ADAMS, DANCER   80200-7/$2.25

Maggie Adams lives in a dancer's world of strained muscles and dirty toe shoes, sacrifices and triumphs, hard work and tough competition. She has little time for anything but dance, as her family and boyfriend come to learn. Her mother spoils her, her father isn't convinced of her talent, and her boyfriend can't understand why he doesn't come first in her life. But Maggie—gifted and determined—will let nothing stand in her way. "Delightful...Karen Strickler Dean has shown how tough, how demanding a life devoted to dance can be...points out the importance of family and friends." *Los Angeles Times*

BETWEEN DANCES:
Maggie Adams Eighteenth Summer   79285-0/$2.25

In this sequel to MAGGIE ADAMS, DANCER, Maggie has just graduated from high school and is sure to win an apprentice-ship with the San Francisco City Ballet Company. But on her 18th birthday, her hopes are devastated; her close friend, Lupe, wins the only female opening. However, Lupe leaves the ballet company to marry the man she loves—a decision Maggie can't understand. But when Maggie finds herself faced with a similar choice, she realizes just how difficult it is to make the decision between love and dance.

MARIANA   78345-2/$1.95

15-year-old Mariana is growing into a strong and graceful dancer. But a handsome piano student comes into her life, and Mariana finds herself torn between two dreams when she falls in love for the first time—and risks undoing all her years of rigorous ballet training.

**From the Emmy Award
Winning Team of
Bruce and Carole Hart**

SOONER OR LATER   55079 $1.95

A Major Television Motion Picture starring Rex Smith ("You Take My Breath Away")

When 13-year-old Jessie falls for Michael Skye, the handsome, 17-year-old leader of The Skye Band, she's sure he'll never be interested in her if he knows her true age . . . and she pretends to be older. But Jessie realizes she has to tell him the truth sooner or later. Because she is ready for her first love, and—much to her surprise—Michael is ready for her.

WAITING GAMES   79012 $2.50

Jessie loves Michael more than ever. But they are at a new stage in their relationship—and he wants more from her. Just as Jessie is trying to decide what to do, her parents announce that the family is going away for the entire summer. Jessie is shattered at being torn away from Michael. And before she leaves she must make a decision. How much is she willing to share with Michael—the man she's sure she'll love forever?

AVON Original **Flare Paperbacks**

Available wherever paperbacks are sold or directly from the publisher. Include $1.00 per copy for postage and handling: allow 6-8 weeks for delivery. Avon Books, Dept BP, Box 767, Rte 2, Dresden, TN 38225.

Hart 1-82

FLARE NOVELS
FROM BESTSELLING AUTHOR
NORMA KLEIN

BREAKING UP 59972-4/$2.25
When 15-year-old Ali Rose goes to visit her father and his new wife in California, she expects a carefree summer. But Ali's summer turns out to be a time of impossible decisions. She is forced to make a choice in the custody battle between her divorced parents and between her possessive best friend and a new love.

IT'S NOT WHAT 59253-3/$1.95
YOU'D EXPECT
Carla and Oliver, 14-year-old twins, are angry and confused about their father's decision to go to New York to work on his novel—and leave the family behind. But as the summer progresses, Carla and Oliver are presented with more perplexing problems. Together they come to understand their parent's unsteady marriage—and their own young adulthood.

MOM, THE WOLFMAN 59998-8/$1.95
AND ME
Brett—sensible and thoroughly modern—loves the unconventional life she leads. But when her unmarried mom meets an attractive, unattached man with an Irish wolfhound, Brett begins to worry that she may do something crazy—like get married! This novel, which was made into a television movie was called "a remarkable book" by *The New York Times*.

TAKING SIDES   60004-8/$1.95
When their parents are divorced, Nell and her five-year-old brother, Hugo go to live with their father. There are many adjustments to be made and Nell sometimes wishes for a more normal life. But she gradually grows to accept her lifestyle, and, finally, she discovers it is possible to love both her parents at the same time.

SUNSHINE   80341-0/$2.25
Jacquelyn Helton died at the age of 20 from a rare form of bone cancer. Her story tells what it's like to die, to leave a husband and two-year-old daughter behind and to try to squeeze every ounce of love and happiness into a sadly short period of time. An acclaimed CBS television movie, SUNSHINE "bursts with the joy and fulfillment of living."
                                    Los Angeles Times

Available wherever paperbacks are sold or directly from the publisher. Include $1.00 per copy for postage and handling; allow 6-8 weeks for delivery. Avon Books, Dept BP, Box 767, Rte 2, Dresden, TN 38225.